LUCY WOOD is the critically acclaimed author of ~~Diving Belles~~, a ~~collection of short stories~~ based on Cornish folklore, and *Weathering*, a debut novel about mothers, daughters and ghosts. She has been longlisted for the Dublin Literary Award and the Dylan Thomas Prize, shortlisted for the Edge Hill Prize, and was runner-up in the BBC National Short Story Award. She has also received a Betty Trask Award, a Somerset Maugham Award and a Holyer an Gof Award. *Weathering* was named as one of *The New York Times'* 100 Notable Books of 2016. She lives in Cornwall.

Praise for *The Sing of the Shore*:

'Rain-drenched, windswept and haunted – this is how I felt as I read *The Sing of the Shore*. Wood's is a Cornwall filled with uneasy spirits, both living and dead, but that also welcomed me in with wry gossip and knowing looks. Absorbing, beautiful, and deeply uncanny, this collection soaked me through and will linger in my bones'   ZOE GILBERT, author of *Folk*

'Heart-thumping miniature thrillers … There's an uncanny, delicate quality to much of Wood's prose that belies how diffi-cult this kind of writing is to pull off'   *Guardian*

'The sounds of the sea and the weather ripple through these eerie, exceptional stories set in a Cornwall that is, by turns, moody and melancholy, wonder-filled and woebegone'

~~ARTHUR BARRY~~, *Daily Mail*

'Mesmerising short-story collection … the writing is so good it is hard to resist' LEAF ARBUTHNOT, *Sunday Times*

'She's better than ever' JON MCGREGOR, *Guardian*

'Elegant new collection of stories … Every figure is wonderfully observed, their lives made poignant and moving in a few brief pages' LAMORNA ASH, *TLS*

'She constructs a vivid, uneasy fictional geography of modern Cornwall' JONATHAN MCALOON, *Spectator*

'*The Sing of the Shore* shows Lucy Wood at the top of her considerable game'

PATRICK GALE, author of *Notes from an Exhibition*

'The stories of *The Sing of the Shore* continue to resonate long after you have closed its covers, and form a remarkably fine collection, beautiful and unsettling' *Shiny New Books*

'These haunting, elegiac stories capture bleak moments of unfulfilled lives' *S Magazine, Sunday Express*

ALSO BY LUCY WOOD

Diving Belles
Weathering

The Sing of the Shore

Lucy Wood

4th ESTATE • London

4th Estate
An imprint of HarperCollins*Publishers*
1 London Bridge Street
London SE1 9GF

www.4thEstate.co.uk

First published in Great Britain in 2018 by 4th Estate
This 4th Estate paperback edition published in 2019

1

Supported using public funding by
**ARTS COUNCIL
ENGLAND**

Kind permission to reproduce an excerpt from *A Glossary of
Cornish Sea-Words* by Robert Morton Nance (1963) granted by
the Federation of Old Cornwall Societies.

A catalogue record for this book is
available from the British Library

ISBN 978-0-00-819340-9

Printed and bound in Great Britain by
CPI Group (UK) Ltd, Croydon, CR0 4YY

MIX
Paper from
responsible sources
FSC **FSC™ C007454**
www.fsc.org

This book is produced from independently certified FSC paper
to ensure responsible forest management.

For more information visit: www.harpercollins.co.uk/green

For Ellie and Georgina

The sing of the shore:
the sound made by waves breaking, varying with the nature
of the shore – sand, pebbles, boulders, scarped cliff, or reefs
and ledges of rock – and thus giving the experienced fisherman
an indication of his position when fog or darkness make land
invisible

– FROM *A Glossary of Cornish Sea-Words*

BY ROBERT MORTON NANCE

Contents

Home Scar   1

The Dishes   27

Dreckly   51

One Foot in Front of the Other   75

Way the Hell Out   83

Salthouse   91

Flotsam, Jetsam, Lagan, Derelict   109

The Life of a Wave   123

Standing Water   143

A Year of Buryings   151

Cables   169

The Sing of the Shore   177

By-the-Wind Sailors   215

Acknowledgements   229

Home Scar

THE SEA WAS WHAT his father called a cowshitty sea – a brown-ish, algae green, that meant it would be good fishing, even though it sounded like it would be bad fishing. But when he said something was bullshit, like the landlord raising the rent, or not fixing the oven, or mentioning that he might put the flat up for sale, then that was definitely something bad. Except when he was in the pub, in a group, and then it could be said and the laughter would be low and raucous as seagulls. To Ivor, it was all in the same murky category as words like restive – Ivor is a very restive boy, his teacher would say into the phone, is everything alright? Apparently that didn't mean that he was calm and easy.

The beach had been scraped and dragged by the winter storms. It was almost March now and where there had been sand there were stones, and where there had been stones there were channels that kept their water long after the tide had gone back out.

Crystal and Gull Gilbert were throwing stones at a limpet on a rock. The rock was covered in a rind of barnacles and there were anemones deep in the cracks; dark red and glistening like sweets.

Crystal picked up a handful of stones and threw them. One of them hit the limpet but it didn't move. She went up and pressed her hand against it. The limpet grated a few milli-metres across the rock. 'That one up there looks empty,' she said. She was pushing the limpet, but staring at a house on the cliff.

'Let's do something else,' Ivor said. The week billowed and sagged around them, like a tent that might stay up, or might at any moment collapse. It was a school holiday. They'd already wrecked Crystal's TV and been forced out of Gull Gilbert's house by his brother, who had a girl hidden in his sour, dim bedroom. Ivor had seen her feet sticking out from under the bed.

He put his hand in one of the pools. Sea gooseberries rolled in the wind, scattering like a smashed chandelier. The ripples in the pool were dark and bright. Crystal's hair was the same dark, dry colour as charcoal – you could rub your hand over it and get an electric shock. Sometimes it got tangled and clumps had to be cut off with scissors. She was the biggest person in their class, bigger even than Gull Gilbert, and could put a safety pin through the skin on her elbow. Last year she'd pushed over a teacher.

2

'We've been in there already,' Gull Gilbert said. He picked up a stone with two hands and swung it through the air. There were blotchy freckles on his wrists and neck. He never wore a coat. He picked up another stone. He was frowning like he always did when he was concentrating. He would throw for hours until he hit his target in exactly the way he wanted. When he was concentrating, you knew exactly what he was doing. When he wasn't, anything could happen.

'We haven't,' Crystal said.

'Let's go back into town,' Ivor said. There was an indent in the rock, shallow and easy to miss at first, where the limpet had been before it moved. It was exactly the same size as the limpet's shell and it had the same rough curves, the same fluted edge.

'I want to go in that one.' Crystal pushed her foot in the sand and turned a fast, lumbering pirouette.

Gull Gilbert put his stone down slowly.

Ivor closed his eyes and leaned into the wind. If he did it right, it was like falling without ever hitting the ground. The cold found its way through his jumper, puckering the folds of skin. Goosebumps, goose barnacles, sea gooseberries. There weren't as many geese as there used to be, his father said. He had mended Ivor's jumper with lumpy stitches.

They'd already tried most of the other empty houses. There was the white one with the blue door, which had a porcelain doll on the windowsill that stared at them with its cracked face. The ceilings were streaked with yellow and the whole place smelled like a stale tin of biscuits. They would prise up slates

3

and scratch their names underneath, pick at the bare walls until the plaster flaked off like confetti, and lie on the stiff, damp beds. But this time all the lights were on and someone was standing in the kitchen.

The big house with the red roof had people in it as well – there were bags and suitcases by the door, and the sound of voices and laughing. Sometimes they would go in there, sit on the leather chairs and read the tourist leaflets, then open all the cupboards to see if anyone had forgotten to pack anything – they'd found watches, cigarettes, a silky dressing gown that they'd taken turns wearing. Once, the oven had been left on by accident and Gull Gilbert had turned it off, then, after a moment, turned it back on again.

And then, just as they were testing the door of the stone house, the cleaning man had driven up and shouted something. Crystal had run first, then Gull Gilbert, Ivor struggling behind, his armpits streaming, that shivery almost-laughing feeling in his throat and bladder.

The wind dropped and Ivor tipped forward. The sand creaked under his knees like polystyrene. He opened his eyes. The others had already gone. Their footprints crossed the beach, sloppy as leftover cereal. Water rose up and filled each print, stretching them until they disappeared.

They were circling the house when he got up there. Gull Gilbert was trying the front windows, which faced out to sea and were rimed with salt.

Ivor lifted the doormat and looked under. There was nothing there. Sometimes the keys would be in locked boxes on the wall and you had to know the right combination to get in. There were a thousand different combinations, maybe a million. You could try all day and never get it right. Sometimes people left back doors open. Sometimes you could slide old windows down. Or, if you watched long enough, you might see someone hiding a spare key – behind flowerpots, underneath paving slabs, pushed into the thumb of a glove.

He let the doormat drop back down. What they should do was go into town and get some of those coins out of the wishing well. Then they could sit in a café and order drinks and talk about things, even though he couldn't imagine what drinks they would order, or what things they would talk about.

There was a grinding sound and Gull Gilbert swore. The grinding got louder, then, suddenly, Crystal was standing inside the house.

Ivor went round the back. One of the windows was open – the bottom pane had been forced up and there were splinters of paint and wood on the ground. A saucepan crashed onto the floor somewhere, something kept clicking, there was a drift of gas, then nothing.

He climbed in. The house was cold in that deep, quiet way that meant no one had been inside it for a long time. The window went into the bathroom, then the bathroom went out to a narrow hallway lined with pictures. The pictures showed the same three faces over and over – a man and a woman and a boy who was sometimes a baby, sometimes older.

Gull Gilbert was methodically checking each room. 'There's a load of crud in here,' he said. 'Shoes and shit.' He disappeared into the bathroom, then came back out. 'Where's all those small, wrapped-up soaps?'

'It's not one of those places,' Ivor told him.

'What?'

'Where different people come every week. It's not one of those places,' Ivor said. He kept looking at the pictures on the wall. The family were eating together round the table, they were walking outside on the cliffs, they were sitting on a rug on the beach.

'There's weird food they've left behind back here,' Crystal shouted.

Gull Gilbert jerked round, almost skidded. 'I'll pay you to eat it.'

'How much?'

Crystal was in the kitchen. The fridge was open and there was a pot of something on the table that smelled bitter and plasticky, like dentists' gloves. She was chewing on a strand of her hair. Whenever she got it cut, there would be a smooth, pale strip of skin on the back of her neck. In the lunch queue, she'd slipped her hand up Ivor's sleeve and held her palm against his shoulder blade. But that skin had been rough and almost scorching.

'How much?' Crystal said again.

Gull Gilbert went over and examined the food. 'Twelve,' he told her.

'When?'

'Tomorrow.'

'You won't have it tomorrow.'

6

Gull Gilbert was pacing the room with long strides. 'I'll pay you every week. Over the summer.'

Crystal reached out towards the pot, then stopped. 'I won't be here in the summer.'

The sea sounded like gunshots through the house. 'Again?' Ivor said, too loudly.

The last time Crystal had gone away, it had been to Cyprus, and it had been for a whole year. Before that, it was somewhere he'd forgotten the name of, for six months. One day she was here, the next she wasn't. It was because her parents worked at the Dishes. They had to go to places where there were other Dishes. She'd been born on an island called Ascension, which meant going up in the air and not coming back down.

'How long for?' he said, quieter this time.

'I'll pay you two pounds right now,' Gull Gilbert said.

Crystal's hand went back towards the pot. 'Three,' she said.

Ivor took a step backwards then turned and kept walking until he was out of the room and in the hallway. Something moved in the glass of one of the pictures and he glanced round quickly, then realised it was just himself. He went into the front room and stood by the window. The sea was rock-coloured and surging. There was the familiar feeling in his chest – tight and untethered at the same time, like a straining balloon. They said it was his asthma and gave him an inhaler to use. But asthma was what happened when you'd been running or fighting, it wasn't what happened when you were standing still.

Along the window there were yoghurt pots crammed with sand and shells and bits of smooth blue glass. The bits of glass were so small; it would have taken a long time to find them all.

Gull Gilbert might leave too. Then he wouldn't have to move up to the big school next year like everyone else. Any time he felt like it, he could wave goodbye to his grandparents and go and live with his father, who worked in a town with shops so huge you could walk around in them all day, and eat in them, and stay in them until it was night.

Ivor reached out and gently knocked each pot over, until the sand and the stones and the glass spilled down the wall and onto the floor.

He didn't know how long he'd been standing there before he saw Crystal and Gull Gilbert outside. They were running towards the path, shouting back at him that it was boring, it was a bit bollocks. They were going back into town. What they wanted was helium, cheap biscuits from the out-of-date food shop, that sticky hairspray that smelled like the bottle of drink they'd found washed up on the beach last summer.

His father was kneeling in the grass by the front door. The road out the front was full of parked cars, cats sleeping against wheels, a skip loaded with rubble and cracked sinks and flower-pots. At the bottom of the street there was a wedge of sea, strung between the houses like a wrinkled sheet.

Ivor opened the gate and his father looked up and then back down again. There was a bike strewn in pieces around him –

handlebars, wheels, a seat with a split like the skin of a tomato. His father picked up the chain and held it for a moment. There was a bottle of oil on the grass and oil on his hands.

Ivor pulled at an oily dandelion. 'Why are you doing that?' he said.

'Fixing it.' When his father was kneeling like that, the top of his head showed through his hair and there were bright blue veins, so thin they looked like they might break, behind his ears. But when he looked up there was the same face as ever – creased eyes from squinting into the sun, cheeks that scraped when they touched against Ivor's, the bent top tooth like a door off its hinges. There was a hole in his eyebrow with a ring in it, which he'd got when he was sixteen, just before Ivor was born.

'Why are you?' Ivor said.

His father ran his hand down the back of his neck. 'Dean's brother asked if I could. He's paying me.'

'Can you?'

'There's loads of bikes when you think about it,' his father said. 'Think how many bikes there are that need fixing.'

Ivor ripped at the dandelion. 'Can you?'

'Almost everyone has a bike. They always need fixing, don't they.'

The window in the flat above them opened and TV and laughing came out. A seagull lifted itself off the roof and circled the chimney, barking sharply.

Ivor leaned against the wall until the pebbles dug into his spine. His father was turning the bike wheel with his finger.

Ivor took his inhaler out of his bag and puffed it. He moved his arm into the shape of a gun and aimed at the seagull, bang bang. He would never hurt a seagull. Bang. If his father could fix the bike then there would be a lot more bikes he could fix, almost everyone had a bike. But if he stopped turning the wheel, got up and went inside without saying anything, then he couldn't fix the bike.

Then it would be like that time the hotel management changed and they could stick their longer shifts with no extra pay up their arses. And when the car park closed where his father gave out tickets and they played guess who would be fattest when they stepped out of their car. Or when everyone stopped coming on his walking tours because whenever he took people out onto the headland, where the cliff suddenly sloped and there was the beach for three miles and the rocks in horseshoes and waves galloping in and everything was silver, his father would just stand there shaking his head and say, fucking delectable, absolutely fucking delectable.

The bike wheel kept turning like it was a clock slowly being wound.

'Did you ring Mev yet?' Ivor said.

'Did I do what?'

'Did you ring Mev.'

Still the wheel kept turning, grating softly each time.

'She said she needed to know,' Ivor said.

'What?'

'About the restaurant. She said she needed to know.' Before Mev moved away, she used to stay over, and in the mornings

Ivor was allowed to get in their bed and keep sleeping. But that was last year, when he was a little kid.

'I know,' his father said. 'I told you that.'

'Why don't we?'

'What?'

'Go and live with Mev and work in her restaurant.'

The church bells near the beach tolled five times. 'That's a hundred miles away, Ivor.'

It was almost dark. If his father could fix the bike, there would be potatoes frying in oil and tomatoes sliced with sugar on them. 'So?' Ivor said.

And for dessert they would shake up cans of cream and spray them straight into their mouths.

The bike wheel went round and round.

His father got up, put the screwdriver down carefully on the grass and went into the house without saying a word.

Ivor pushed the window up until his wrists burned. The frame shuddered and jammed, then finally opened.

Below him, the cliff was slumped and worn, the rock underneath pale as a shinbone. Green waves crumbled onto the beach, then pulled back against the stones like a rasping intake of breath. A surfer drifted in the darker water.

He climbed inside, checked the window wouldn't fall shut behind him, then checked again. When he looked back out, the surfer had gone.

It was colder than before. The quiet was thick as dust. The floorboards creaked softly under his feet. That morning he'd put on his coat, found the shopping list and money his father had left next to the sink, and walked down the road into town. He'd got to the shop, picked up a basket, then put the basket down and kept walking until the road turned to the path along the cliffs, and then the house, and then the loose back window.

He moved slowly through each room, opening empty drawers and cupboards, running his fingers over a shelf of maps and books, a crackling bunch of dried flowers. There were patterned plates and glasses that looked like they'd hardly been used, and bowls that were too small for anything. There were leaflets heaped by the door and he picked some up, read something about window cleaning, something about gardening services, then he put them back down where he'd found them.

There were three pairs of sandals by the front door, three raincoats, three wetsuits folded over hangers. Ivor looked them over one by one. Nothing had sand on it, or mud, or crusts of salty rain. There was no torn and snapped umbrella, no piles of old newspaper, no takeaway pots flattened and ready for the outside bin. There were no tangled keys, no stacks of bills hidden behind the microwave. He looked under every bed but there were no cardboard boxes, reinforced with gaffer tape, waiting.

Nothing moved except Ivor. No clocks ticked. There were three yellow chairs round one of the windows and he sat in each one, then got up and watched the dents he'd made spring slowly back to smoothness. He opened and closed the curtains.

He turned on the lamp. His trainers left faint treads of sand. There were some clothes in the small bedroom – not many, just a few shirts and a jumper – and he unfolded each one, studied them carefully, then folded them back up, matching the creases exactly.

In the bathroom, he opened the cabinet above the sink and took out the bottles and jars. He opened the lids one by one and dipped his fingers into the creams, then scooped up talcum powder, leaving behind shallow indents and the half-moon shapes of his nails. He tipped up a bottle and white tablets fell onto his palm. When he tipped them back in, one tablet stuck to his skin. It was small and perfectly round. He thought about swallowing it, then shook his head and lifted his hand to drop it back in. But now that the thought had appeared, there was nothing else he could do. It was like locking and unlocking the door three times, or touching the wing mirrors of every red car.

His breath fogged up the mirror and he wiped it away with his sleeve, but it stayed on there for a long time after he'd left.

Every day his father would go fishing. His lines and nets were always by the door. He would leave early, depending on the tide, and there would be the sound of him in the kitchen, packing his kit, the thump of the car boot. He would hum that song he liked where the tune went so low it was as if his chest was vibrating.

When he came in to say goodbye he would put his hand on the top of Ivor's head and it would be warm and smell like bait. Ivor would pretend to be asleep. When he went downstairs, his breakfast would be on the table: milkshake, cereal that had soaked up everything, a plate of crackers to dip in. His father always said he'd only be gone a few hours, but he was never only gone for a few hours.

Ivor came down off the cliffs and glanced back once more in the direction of the house. There were bits of chipped paint on his hands from the window, and bits of talcum powder under his nails. He rubbed them off and crossed the beach towards the road. His father was down at the edge of the water. His silhouette was like a hawthorn bending. His line was arched over the sea and there were a couple of cans by his feet.

'Did you get the shopping?' his father said. Cold radiated off him, and he pulled the hood of his sweatshirt up against it.

Ivor stood as close as he could without knocking anything. The sky over the sea had turned dark yellow, like a very old piece of paper.

The line tensed and began to buckle, and his father gave his can to Ivor and put his hand on the reel.

'I forgot,' Ivor told him. He took his father's other hand and blew on each stiff knuckle.

His father played out the line. The bones in his fingers made popping noises under Ivor's mouth. 'Remember when your breath smelled like those onion crisps for a week?' his father said. 'I almost took you to the doctor.'

'Remember when you ate that whole sweetcorn and your beard smelled like butter?'

The line tensed some more, and it was important to watch it, and bring it in slowly. Now his father needed both hands.

The line went tighter and tighter, then slackened. His father took the can back and sipped it. 'I'll catch us something,' he said. He still held the record for catching the biggest fish in town.

The dark yellow turned to dark blue. A ship flashed on the horizon. Somewhere the oystercatchers whistled and scolded like boiling kettles.

'How about this then,' his father said.

Sometimes Ivor didn't think his father really even minded if he caught a fish or not, because then he could just stand out there all day, all night even, and sip his beer and listen to the sea, until the mist came in and rose up around his feet, and everyone else had gone home a long time ago, and their lights would be on along the streets, and their curtains would start to close, and cooking smells would come out, and it would just be him and Ivor left on the beach, waiting and watching the line.

Crystal ate chips like a seagull – she held one up in her mouth, then dropped it straight down her throat. She sat cross-legged by the swings, the beach sloping down in front of them. Ivor dug in the sandy grass with his fingers.

'We should be sitting on a rug,' he said.

'A what?'

'A rug. We should probably be sitting on one.'

The tide was just going out and the stones were still wet – they looked like they were splashed with blue paint. A dog ran up, soaked and quivering, holding a crushed barbecue as if it was a stick to throw. Behind them, Gull Gilbert swung standing up, the bent chains clanking.

'Why?' Crystal said.

Ivor dug his fingers in deeper. 'I don't know.'

Crystal held her chips against her chest until the dog went away. 'You'd have to know you were going to sit on it, then carry it down especially.'

'I suppose.'

'How would you know?'

'What?'

'If you were definitely going to sit on it,' Crystal said. Her weird lacy skirt was rucked and there was sand high up on her legs.

The swing behind them thumped as Gull Gilbert rode it like a bull at a rodeo.

'I don't know,' Ivor said. His chest started to tighten. 'Maybe you're just supposed to know.'

Crystal ate another chip. Sometimes she would pass one to Ivor, sometimes she wouldn't. This round he missed out.

'They've probably got them at that house,' he said.

'What house?'

'The one on the cliff.' His fingers hit against a stone and he started digging around it, working it loose. 'We could go there.'

'I'm not walking any more.'

'Tomorrow,' Ivor said. The stone was almost loose; he could nearly get his finger under it. 'All of us.' He thought about the lamps, the three yellow armchairs. He'd gone there again that morning and stood by the kitchen table in the strange, cool quiet, and thought something that wouldn't go away. 'We could stay there.'

Gull Gilbert jumped off the swing and staggered up behind them, his cheeks mottled almost purple. His tracksuit snapped like a flag in the wind. 'That dog's got itself a dead fish,' he said. He dipped his hand in the bag of chips, then skipped away from Crystal's fist. She was known for conjuring the blackest bruises. 'Stay where?' he said.

Ivor's heart raced under his coat. 'At that house.' A hot feeling pushed at the backs of his eyes. If anyone asked why, he didn't know what he would do.

Crystal finished eating, put her arms behind her head and lifted her hips until she was doing the bridge. 'Like, living?' she said. Her hair swung against the ground.

Gull Gilbert scanned the tideline, watching the dog's owner chasing it over the seaweed. 'Do you reckon that dog'll eat that fish?' he said. His eyes looked glassy and far away. Who knew what thoughts were teeming.

Ivor prised the stone out and clenched it in his muddy hand.

The dog started to eat the fish.

Gull Gilbert leaned forward, spat on his palm, said he was in, and shook on it, which was as binding as a triple-signed contract, amen.

When Ivor got home the light was on but his father's shoes weren't on the mat. That meant he was still wearing them, which meant he'd gone straight onto the kitchen sofa. Ivor went in quietly. His father was asleep under the scratchy blanket. Ivor had saved up for that blanket from the gift shop. It didn't seem right that people could sell a blanket that was scratchy, to tourists, or to anyone.

His father murmured something and his cheek twitched. There was a scar under there from when Ivor was three and had bit him. 'Is it right?' his father said. 'Is it right?' He sat up suddenly, opened his eyes and rubbed his hand over his face. 'Christ, Ivor, how long have you been standing there?'

He reached out and pulled him down onto the sofa. It was soft and dusty, and Ivor sneezed, then sneezed again.

The fridge hummed next to his ear. Ivor picked at the fraying cushion threads. 'Did you ring Mev yet?' he said.

His father moved the cushion away. 'You'll tear it.'

'Did you?' Ivor said again.

'These aren't our cushions. If you tear them I'll have to try and buy new ones exactly the same.'

The clock on the oven glowed red – you could see the shapes of all the other numbers behind the lit-up parts.

'Don't you want to be here?' his father said.

Ivor looked around. There was the kitchen, the dark outside the window. 'Here?' he said.

Once, in town, his father had passed someone he used to know from school. His father had recognised the man, Jody, straight away, but it had taken Jody a moment to come up with Ivor's father's name. Jody had been down visiting his parents and now he wanted to go – he kept looking towards his car and nodding in all the wrong places.

Ivor had pulled on his father's hand but his father had kept talking. About the state of the tides, what was biting, the blue shark, the development out the back of town. Remember that party out at the Jennings' place? he said. Remember the ambulance?

Ivor had pulled again at his father's hand, until his father let go. And still Jody kept glancing round and checking his watch, and nodding, until finally he said, I have to get back.

His father had run his hand down his neck and watched him walk away. 'Back,' he said. Then he'd shrugged and walked into the pub. A beer for him and a Coke for Ivor, and those chewy scratchings that were so tough and salty they made your teeth ache.

His father's eyes were closing again.

His phone started to ring in the front room. It rang and rang but he didn't get up to answer it.

'The warehouse might be hiring next week,' he said.

Over went the blanket with its smoky, ketchupy smells. Ivor leaned in and his teeth were against his father's cheek, and his father's hand came up and smoothed and smoothed, like he did with the fish he caught when they were thrashing and gleaming.

19

Ivor got to the house first. It was late afternoon and the sky was dark, the cliffs silhouetted like breaching whales. He'd told his father he was staying at Gull's and would be back in the morning. The town glinted in the distance, supermarket floodlights bright as haloes.

It was raining and he put his bags down and pushed at the window. It didn't move. He leaned forward and pushed harder. The frame was wet and heavy. It shook but didn't budge.

He ran round the side of the house, tried the other windows, then rattled the front door. The rain came down in sharp pieces. He looked towards the town, then back at the house. He shoved the door, then leaned all his weight against it. Something gave and he shoved again. A gap appeared and he forced it with his shoulder. The door jolted open. The wood around the lock was spongy and on his way in he pushed the screws of the metal plate until they nestled back in place.

When the others arrived he met them at the front. Crystal was carrying a rucksack. Gull Gilbert had brought nothing.

They stood inside, too close, Crystal's arm pressed against Ivor's. She smelled like apples and petrol and she was wearing lace-up boots that reached almost to her knees, and a pyjama jacket with clouds on it. Gull Gilbert had slicked down the sides of his hair.

Ivor's cheeks were hot. Everyone was just standing in the open doorway, waiting.

Gull Gilbert prodded Ivor's bags with his foot. 'What's in these?'

'Nothing,' Ivor said. It was just the food he'd brought. There was a packet of crackers, cheese he'd cut off a bigger piece, half a carton of orange juice, a tin of soup, eggs although he had no idea what to do with eggs. Also three cans of beer he'd found lurking at the back of the fridge.

When he'd packed it, he'd thought there was too much – he'd almost taken out the cheese – but now everything looked small and awful. Any moment now, Gull Gilbert's lip would twist and everything would crumble.

A handful of rain flung itself across the wall. Gull Gilbert reached out and closed the door. 'We should get all that in the fridge,' he said.

They went into the kitchen. Ivor put the eggs in the cupboard, then took them out and put them in the fridge. He thought the orange juice should go in the fridge door, the soup on a shelf. He spent a long time deciding, even though he knew he'd be getting it all out again in a minute.

Crystal went to the sink and ran the tap. She opened all the cupboards and looked inside, got out plates and slammed them down on the table. Then she picked them up and placed them gently. Then she pursed her lips, crossed her arms over her chest and pretended to smoke. Finally she slumped down over the table with her head in her hands. 'What are we supposed to do?' she said.

Gull Gilbert pulled out a chair, sat down, and got up again. The chair screeched against the floor and made everyone flinch.

He opened the fridge. 'We should have a drink,' he said.

'Now?' Ivor said.

'It's Friday, isn't it?'

The cans opened with a hiss. When Ivor drank, all he felt was very cold. He realised that the lights were off. He clicked them on and the kitchen turned orange. The room appeared in the black window, three faces staring back in.

He went out into the hall and looked at the pictures. In one of them, the table was laid with all the different types of cutlery, and the food was on mats in the middle. He went back into the kitchen and started laying out knives and forks and spoons, then he opened the soup and glooped it into a pan.

Gull Gilbert had one leg up on the table. His fingers drummed. 'We need to turn the lights off,' he said. He tipped his can and drained it to the dregs. His voice sounded huskier, as if his throat was very dry.

'I want the lights on,' Ivor said. He tipped his can up until the bubbles burned his throat. The taste was getting better, or maybe his mouth was going numb.

'Someone will see us,' Gull Gilbert said. He got up and clicked off the lights. The kitchen plunged into gloom. He sat back down and up went his leg. He stared at Crystal's beer. 'Are you going to finish that?' he said.

Ivor got up and drew the curtains, glanced at Gull Gilbert, then turned on the lamp in the corner. He took another long drink, then clicked the burner under the pan of soup. Nothing happened. He clicked it again.

'The gas is broken,' Crystal said. 'I tried it before.'

'Shitting frick,' Ivor said.

'You have to hit something when you say that,' Crystal told him. 'Then you have to go and lock yourself in the bathroom.'

Ivor drank some more beer, then spooned the soup into bowls. There were only a few cold spoonfuls in each one but he laid them out anyway, then the cheese. 'Someone else could help,' he said.

Gull Gilbert got up and brought over the crackers and spread them across a plate. He took out the eggs and looked at them, then put one down in front of each of them. 'I'm not hungry yet,' he said.

Ivor looked at his watch. 'I think this is the time we're supposed to eat.' He cut the cheese into slices and gave them out. The rain hit the windows with clinking sounds. 'We should have a conversation,' he said.

'Us?' Crystal said. She had taken more than her share of the crackers.

'Say something,' Ivor said.

Gull Gilbert was pushing his spoon around his bowl. 'Did you make this soup yourself, Ivor?'

Crystal snorted into her bowl. 'Why are you talking in that voice?'

Gull Gilbert's spoon clattered down. 'He said we had to have a conversation.' His leg wouldn't stop drumming.

Ivor poured out the orange juice, which looked too thick. He couldn't remember how long it had been open. 'Don't actually drink this,' he said as he passed it round.

Crystal took hers and started drinking.

'I said don't drink it.' Ivor tried to slow his breathing. There was sand everywhere. He should have got everyone to take their shoes off. He crouched down and started scooping it up into his hand.

'Where are we going to sleep?' Crystal said.

Gull Gilbert leaned back in his chair. 'Depends,' he said. 'Do you snore?'

'How would I know?'

Ivor crawled under the table. The sand was everywhere. The grains he'd already picked up kept scattering out of his hand. 'I think we should take our shoes off,' he said. He followed the gritty trail out into the middle of the kitchen.

Gull Gilbert was staring at Crystal. 'You'll have to sleep in my room.'

Crystal stared back, harder. 'Why?'

Gull Gilbert's eyes shifted away, he put his leg down from the table, got up and started pacing. He pointed to her beer. 'Are you going to finish that?'

'I already did.'

He reached out and shook it to check, then crushed the empty can in his fist.

Ivor tipped the sand in the bin then sat back down. No one had finished their soup. Gull Gilbert was circling the edges of the room, wall to wall to wall.

Ivor took a spoonful and raised it to his mouth, but he couldn't do it. He pushed his bowl away. His spoon had rust on the handle. His stomach made a thin, hollow noise. 'Soon we have to go and sit in the armchairs,' he said.

Crystal was moving her chair closer. Ivor sat very still. What he was probably meant to do was lean in to her and smell her hair, like his father used to do to Mev.

His breathing was so fast and shallow it was as if he couldn't catch up with it.

'You took too many crackers,' Ivor told her.

Crystal stopped moving for a moment, then tipped her chair back and swung on its spindly legs. She started humming something fast and looping.

Gull Gilbert turned on the TV. There was someone on there doing a magic trick with cards, but you could see where she'd tucked the spare ones in her pocket. He picked up the remote and changed the channel. A zebra was running through a wide river. He changed the channel again and there was a crowd of people. He flicked it again and again.

The room was cold and dark. The blue from the TV and the orange from the lamp cast a strange, underwater light. Crystal's chair was almost at the point where it would snap. Gull Gilbert was staring at the screen with unfocused eyes. His hair had sprung up slowly from under its layer of gel. He kept moving from channel to channel without stopping, one image blurred into the next; there was a voice, then music, then more voices. The zebra was still in the river, the crowd of people was getting bigger. The magician's hidden cards fell on the ground like leaves from a wilting plant.

Ivor pushed his plate off the table. It slid across the shiny wood and kept sliding, then seemed to pause for a moment before it hit the floor and shattered.

Crystal stopped tipping. Gull Gilbert blinked and looked around.

Ivor picked up his glass. It glinted in the TV's light. He held it out over the floor, then he dropped it.

Slowly, Gull Gilbert's elbow moved towards his plate. It teetered on the edge of the table, then broke with a hard clunking sound across his shoes.

Crystal picked up her plate, licked off the last crumbs, and dropped it. She got up and kicked her chair over behind her.

Then they all picked up their stupid eggs, raised them in the air, and smashed them into a million glorious pieces.

Ivor finally caught up with his own breath. His hand touched against Crystal's hand and he tried to make it mean that he would miss her when she wasn't there. Even though he didn't know if you could say that just with hands.

The sea paced with its heavy boots through the house. If you listened closely, you could tell how high the tide was, and what kind of waves were breaking. Ivor's father could walk out the front door and know that the waves were mushy, or that it was low tide and the waves were clean as a damn whistle.

Ivor picked up his can and rubbed the back of his neck. Later, but not now, he would clean up the house, and whoever came in next, whenever they came in next, would find, what? Not anything worth mentioning really: a scatter of crumbs, a few missing plates, a lamp that had been left on by mistake, sand in the floorboards, a smudge of breath on the bathroom mirror that could have been anyone's.

The Dishes

THE BABY WAS TEETERING on the edge of speech. Bru, she would say. Da Da Da. She had a way of looking at him as if she knew. Her forehead would furrow and her eyes would go dark as oil. Then he would pick her up and carouse around the room, giddy up, giddy up horsey, while the mist pressed against the windows from the sea, wet and dripping like bedding on a line.

They were there for three months. His wife, Lorna, had a temporary posting and they'd been given the use of a small, brick house in a terraced row. Theirs was on the end and it backed onto rough ground: tussocks, bracken, horned sheep sprayed blue and red, as if they were going into battle. Beyond that were fields, hedges tangled like wires, a few lonely farmhouses. The beaches were stony. The trees were not in leaf. In front of the house there was a road that hardly anyone drove along, then a barbed-wire fence with No Entry signs and cameras that pointed in all directions. Behind the fence were the dishes, where his wife went to work every morning and came back later and later into the evening. Sometimes she would have a shift in the middle of the night, and when Jay turned over in bed to hold her, she would be gone.

The dishes were on the edge of the cliff and could be seen for miles – hard white shapes that looked like a chess set waiting to be played. They were data gatherers, listening stations, bigger than the house and smooth and silent. Some were full spheres, some were hexagonal, others hollowed like the dip in an ear. At the centre of each tilted dish there was an antenna that reached upwards, and, sometimes, if Jay watched carefully, he would see them slowly turn, like a flower might, or someone following a voice that no one else could hear.

It was early morning and Lorna had already left. Jay was in the kitchen clearing away the breakfast things. It was cold outside. Rain blew across the road in thin lines. He turned the heating up higher.

The baby was strapped in her chair. He wiped her face with a warm cloth. Her skin was so soft, almost translucent, except for all the dried food stuck to it – it was on her cheeks and on the floor. Some was in her wispy hair. She laughed and squirmed while he wiped around her mouth, then puckered her lips and blew a bubble. Jay crouched down and tried to blow one too but it didn't work and he ended up drooling down one corner of his mouth. The baby laughed and blew another one.

'How are you doing that?' he said.

'Hamna fla,' the baby told him.

'Oh, OK,' Jay said. 'I thought you were doing it a different way.'

He picked up the plates and put them in the sink, then ran the hot water until the washing liquid foamed up. He plunged his hands in and his wrists went red.

'What do you want to do today?' he said.

The baby banged her hands against her tray.

'Do you want to go out anywhere?'

She banged again.

'Or we could play that xylophone game you seem to like so much.'

She kept banging.

'Bang your hands if you've got food in your hair.'

She kept banging.

'Bang your hands if you woke me up five times last night.'

She banged again.

'Bang your hands if you think I'm the best.'

She stopped banging.

Jay ran more hot water and swiped plate after plate with the cloth, until they were all stacked on the draining board. He liked washing up now – the hot water, the steam, how, when he rinsed out a tin of tomatoes, he pretended there'd been a shark attack. He liked the way the bubbles had bits of colour in them. He would blow them off his hands so that the baby could watch them floating. He hardly ever felt like smashing it all against the wall any more.

He dried his hands and lifted the baby out of the chair and onto her mat. There was an arched bar over it with bells hanging down. They made a dull, jangling noise when she grabbed at them. They sounded like a doorbell and he wished he'd packed her other mat – the one without any bells. They hadn't brought much from home – just a suitcase for him and Lorna and a few boxes of the baby's things. He liked it that this house was small and empty. He could walk around each room seeing nothing that reminded him; just a table, a couple of chairs, a sofa, a wilting pot plant on top of the fridge that he watered every day.

He sat down next to the baby, then got up again. If he sat down he would fall asleep. He had that heavy, dull feeling behind his eyes which pushed down towards his jaw. It had been five times last night; the night before he'd lost count after seven. He straightened the curtains, the chairs, then picked up the cloth and wiped at another weird stain on the floor.

'Was this you?' he said to the baby.

She looked at him, frowning, like it was inappropriate to even ask.

It wasn't even nine o' clock yet.

After a while he noticed the sound of low voices coming through the kitchen wall. He stopped wiping the floor. There it was again: a low murmur of voices.

The wall was thin and connected with next door, but he didn't think there was anyone living there. When they'd arrived there weren't any lights on, and there were no cars parked at the front. The curtains were half-drawn and there was a pile of rubble by the steps – bricks and plaster – that looked as if a room had recently been knocked through.

He couldn't hear what they were saying. He stayed kneeling on the floor. Water dripped off the cloth and pooled next to his leg. The voices rose and fell and then they stopped. The baby let out a cry and he turned to her quickly, thought he heard a door open and close somewhere. The baby cried out again and he picked her up and cupped her warm head with his wet hands.

The front door of the house next door opened then shut with a bang. Jay sat upright in the kitchen chair, where he'd been slumped over a cup of coffee, on the edge of sleep. It was mid-morning the next day. He glanced over at the window. There was a man crossing the road further up, heading towards the dishes. Jay glimpsed the back of his coat before he disappeared through the gates.

An hour later there were footsteps behind the wall, someone ran up the stairs and there was a strange rattling, which might have been curtains closing across their runners.

It was misty again, and too cold to go out. He brought the baby into the living room and turned on the electric fire. Soon the room was warm and fuggy and smelled like burned dust. He brought out a box of toys and emptied it onto the floor. He put the rattle and the fraying bear in front of the baby, then found the spinning top, spun it up, and let it go. It whirled and clinked out tinny music. He spun it up again.

When he got bored he styled the baby's hair into a Mohican.

At lunchtime, someone drove up near the house. The engine revved, idled for a moment, then finally stopped. Jay glanced out. There was a dark blue van parked by the side of the road, in the lay-by in front of the terrace.

He strapped the baby in her chair and put her food in a pan to warm up. 'Mashed peas and potato,' he told her. 'A classic choice.'

'Forofoo,' the baby said. She'd twisted her bib up into her mouth and she was chewing on it.

'It'll be ready in a minute,' Jay told her. 'I just want to make sure it's warm.'

He went over to the sink to wash his hands. He washed them twice, then scrubbed under his nails. He'd read something somewhere about how easy it was to contaminate a baby's food and since then he'd started washing his hands more and more every day. The skin around his nails was sore to the touch.

He dried his hands and filled the baby's bowl with food. He sat down next to her and blew on it to cool it down. 'I just heated this up, now we have to wait for it to cool down,' he said.

'Forofoo,' the baby said, trying to grab the spoon. She took a handful of food and aimed at her mouth, but most of it ran down her wrist and back into the bowl.

After a while the voices started up behind the wall. They were louder this time, closer, although he couldn't make out any actual words. One was deep, the other sounded like a woman's voice. There was a lot of low, drawn-out laughter.

Jay spooned the food into the baby's mouth. He wiped around her lips, then hooked his finger gently inside her cheek to make sure she wasn't storing any of it in there. She'd gone through a stage of doing that – he would find bits of food that she'd kept hidden all night.

She squirmed and sucked at his finger.

'I'm only checking,' he said. 'You have previous, remember?'

The voices came again through the wall. He got up and went over to the window. The van was still there. 'I'll be back in a second,' he said.

He went outside and knocked at next door. He waited, checking his hands for mashed-up peas. What would he say? He didn't know. All he wanted was to speak to someone and not have them say forofoo, or whatever the hell it was, back. But there was no sound from inside. Nothing moved. There were no lights on. Upstairs, the curtains were all drawn. Downstairs, there were net curtains that were frayed and yellowing. He would have to go right up and stare in to see past them. He turned round and looked at the road. The mist had almost covered the dishes. He could only see the one closest to the fence. The metal was dripping. The antenna was tilted towards the road. It almost looked like it was pointing at him. Was it pointing at him? He took a step towards it, then stopped and shook his head. It was pointing upwards, above the houses, like it always did.

He knocked once more, then turned and went back into his own house.

He sat down at the table, spooned up the last bit of the baby's food and put it in her mouth.

The voices started up again, and someone laughed.

He got up so quickly that his chair tipped over. He went back outside and stood there, looking around. There was no one. The van was still parked by the side of the road. It was dusty and there was sand on the tyres.

When he looked out again later, the van had gone.

At night, he watched his wife sleeping. She slept straight away, as soon as she'd checked the baby and got into bed. There were dark smudges under her eyes, as if soot had gathered in a fireplace.

Sometimes she murmured and rolled away from him to the other side of the bed. Sometimes she rolled onto his chest and buried her face in his ribs. She mumbled things he couldn't really hear. 'What?' he would ask her. 'What?' He smoothed back her hair and rubbed her shoulder blades to settle her back into sleep.

'What do you do over there all day?' he asked, but he knew she wasn't allowed to answer.

Often, the pillow would have creased the side of her cheek, and the creases would run into the fine lines that had started to gather around her eyes. When her nightdress rode up, there were lines across her stomach and the tops of her legs, the skin puckering like clay. He couldn't take his eyes off them.

Finally he would fall asleep, but after a few moments he would jolt awake and freeze, sure that he'd been muttering, talking. What had he been saying? What if Lorna had woken up and heard him saying something?

It was only once, it had only happened once. The doorbell had rung and he'd opened it and Lorna had been working, she was always working, and he'd been on his own for such a long time.

The baby had been in the other room. He'd put music on, and afterwards he'd checked and she was deep in sleep, her arms and legs flung outwards, her hand clutching her rabbit, and that warm, sour, milky smell clinging to her which reminded him of the corridors of school many years before; how he used to get lost in the twisting maze of them.

He pressed his ear closer to the kitchen wall. The van had arrived at midday, while Jay was changing the baby. There'd been no sound from next door all morning, and he'd started to think that the van was probably there to do repairs to one of the houses further along the row. Now and again, drilling and hammering would reverberate down the terrace like a heartbeat.

But then someone had run up the stairs. The banister had creaked. A door somewhere further back seemed to shut softly.

He turned away from the wall and back to the baby, who was tipping herself backwards in her chair, trying to get out.

She'd been restless all morning – crying whenever he went out of the room and throwing down toys, but if he picked her up she would go rigid and try to twist out of his arms. Her cheeks were hot and she kept scratching at her belly, and when he rubbed it for her, she just cried again. He offered up her favourite toys – the rabbit, the jangly ball – but she batted them away.

He looked around; saw only the road, the mist, the cliffs, the dishes.

He slumped down in a chair and rested his head on the table. It had not been possible, before, to know that this kind of tiredness existed. He could hardly even lift his head. When he did manage to look up, the baby had slumped down too, in her chair, and she was watching him with her head cocked sideways.

He sat up, then covered his eyes with his hands.

The baby did the same.

He waved his hands, and the baby waved her hands.

She watched him, without blinking, to see what he would do next.

Then someone said 'Ssshhhh' suddenly and loudly from behind the wall.

The baby opened her eyes wide. 'Ssshhh,' she said.

'Ssshhh,' the voice came again from behind the wall.

The baby looked around the room, then back at Jay. 'Ssshhhhh,' she said.

Jay shook his head. 'You don't need to do that,' he told her.

'Ssshhhh,' the baby said again.

Jay got up and went over to her. 'Don't do that.'

She looked at him with her wide, dark eyes.

The sound came again from the wall.

Jay went over and knocked on it, once, twice, loud and hard.

Above him, on the roof, a tile slipped and grated in the wind.

'Sshhhh,' the baby said, quieter this time.

~

There was a swing tied to a branch of a tree at the back of the house. It was small and sturdy, with high sides for a child. Jay had tested it, and tested again, pulling down with all his strength to see if anything gave.

He put the baby in her coat and opened the back door. The misty rain had finally stopped. It was good to feel the wind against his face.

He put the baby in the swing and pushed gently. The chains creaked as they moved against the tree. He pushed and pushed and it was cold and quiet and he thought of nothing except pushing the swing and the wet, salty smell of the fields behind him.

When he looked up at the house, there was someone standing in the window.

He fumbled with the swing, missed the middle of it, and ended up pushing the baby sideways. The swing lurched outwards, rocked, then righted itself.

Jay steadied the chains. It was just his wife, wearing her coat and carrying her bag ready to leave for work. He didn't know how long she'd been standing there; he thought she'd already gone. She was wearing the green scarf he'd bought for her just after they'd first met. He hadn't seen her wearing it for a long time. He raised his hand and waved. Lorna's mouth moved but he couldn't tell what she was saying.

He realised he'd been pushing the swing quite high, and probably harder than he should. The baby was laughing and kicking her legs with each push but now he slowed it down, keeping it low, feeling himself making a show of how careful he was being.

The baby screamed indignantly, but he kept pushing the swing very gently. The next time he looked up, the window was empty, except for the blurred reflection of the swing moving backwards and forwards slowly across the glass.

∼

A phone rang next door. It rang, then cut out, then rang again. No one answered it.

∼

Jay strapped the baby in the pram and pushed her hat further down over her head. She looked up at him and her face creased. Her eyes were exactly the same as Lorna's – sometimes it seemed like she was right there, staring out at him. When Lorna and the baby looked at each other, it was as if something secret passed between them, something that he wasn't allowed to know.

'Ha fa ma?' she asked. Her cheeks were already red in the cold.

'We need to get out of the house,' Jay told her.

'Bada shlam.'

'Yeah, I know. It's bloody cold, but we need to get out of the house.'

He put another blanket over her. She stared out sternly from under all the layers. He tucked the blanket in, then started walking down the road. The pram's wheels sent up spray from the wet tarmac. The road was steep and narrow, with high hedges on both sides. If a car came, there would be nowhere to go. They would have to turn and walk all the way back. But he needed to get out of the house. It had rained for three days in a row – heavy showers that didn't stop. The gutters had spilled over and poured down the windows. They'd stayed in and turned the heaters up high. Small noises had come through the wall: murmurs, footsteps, low laughter. Sometimes he was sure it was just the pipes, or the rain.

There was a thin, raw mist, as if the ground couldn't absorb any more water so the wetness had moved into the air itself. Soon his nose was numb and dripping and his fingers were stiff against the handle of the pram. The road sloped down and small trees twisted on either side, their trunks bright with moss.

It got colder the lower he went into the valley. He could hear the sea somewhere in the distance. Water ran down the road and splashed up his legs. It looked orange, like it was leaking through rusty iron.

The mist thickened into drizzle and he shivered. He crouched down and tucked the baby in tighter. She was making cooing sounds at the gorse, trying to reach out and grab it. He showed her the prickles but she grabbed at it anyway. There was gorse everywhere, like lamps in the hedges. It gave out a sweet, heavy smell.

The drizzle came in waves, sweeping across the tops of the trees, and hanging there like curtains. The road narrowed again. Something moved in the dead leaves under a tree. He walked slowly, checking every bend before carrying on. He came to the bottom of the road and it forked: one way turned into a track that followed a stream, the other seemed to bend inland. He took that one and kept going. There were no road signs, just hedges and fields and the valley below him: the trees huddled like a herd of animals escaping the weather.

'Sa?' the baby asked.

He stroked her damp cheek with his finger.

There was the sound of a motor in the distance, coming closer, and he walked forward to find a wider bit of road. Whatever it was, it was moving fast, the engine revving. He smelled the petrol before he saw it. There was no wider bit of road. He walked back quickly, away from the bend. He crammed the pram in sideways against the hedge, mounting the wheels up on the bank and pressing it in as far as it would go.

It was a dark blue van. It came careening round the corner of the lane and revved past him before he could see who was in it. The wing mirror brushed against him as it went.

40

Jay jumped out and shook his fist at the back of the van. 'You arsehole,' he shouted. 'You irresponsible son-of-a-bitch arsehole.'

He got the pram out of the hedge. The baby had a handful of dried leaves in each fist and was chewing on a stick. He took the stick out of her mouth and crouched down to check she was OK.

'Don't ever repeat what I just said,' he told her.

The baby looked at him, then back down at the leaves she was holding.

He stood in the middle of the road. No one else went past. He saw no one except a farmer, small and faint, walking through a field in the distance. The baby went to sleep. Her hand slackened and the leaves fell out. He turned and started walking back. Soon the dishes rose up in front of him. One of them was pointing down at the valley. It stayed like that all night.

His wife hummed low, monotonous tunes in the shower. She used to sing pop songs, ballads, those deep, soulful ones where she used the showerhead as a microphone, but now she just hummed the same thing over and over, quietly and without stopping, like static on an old radio.

While she was in the shower, music started up behind the wall. It was slow but with a heavy beat that thrummed through the floor. It was coming from somewhere near the kitchen, then it faded and seemed to move into the living room, then down the hall, as if it was in the pipes or the wires.

Jay's heart gave a strange lurch. He banged on the wall. 'Stop it,' he said. He banged again. 'Stop it.'

The music didn't stop. He followed it through the house. It was louder near the bathroom. When he went in, it sounded like it was in the room, low and slow and echoing off the tiles.

He could see Lorna through the steam. She was washing her hair and there was soap and bubbles all over her head. She was humming and her eyes were closed.

There was a thump near the door, and then the sound of breathing only a few inches from where Jay was standing. A cold draught came under the door. Any moment now Lorna would rinse off the soap and take her hands away from her ears and then she would hear.

The breathing got louder. The music surged. Lorna ducked her head under the water and shampoo ran down her neck and onto her shoulders.

He stood in the middle of the room, clenching his hands. His nails dug into his palms. He could tell, even behind the music, the particular way the body would be pressing against the wall.

Stop, he said silently. Stop it.

Lorna shook her wet hair and turned off the shower.

The music stopped.

She opened her eyes and when she saw Jay she let out a faint cry and put her hand on her chest, looking at him for a moment as if she didn't recognise him at all.

~

The phone rang from behind the wall. It rang and then it cut out, then it rang again. Still no one answered it.

~

It was lunchtime and Jay was cleaning up. The baby had woken him every few hours in the night and he kept knocking things onto the floor – cups, bits of food. The baby would lean down out of her chair and try to help him pick them up, then almost topple out, so he would straighten her, and then she would do it again, clapping her sticky hands.

Soon Lorna would be home and he would start cooking something for dinner.

He ran the sink full of hot water. It was cold in the house, his hands were cold and he was looking forward to dipping them in.

An engine revved suddenly and he looked up just in time to see the van speed away past the window. The tyres left a burning smell on the air.

He picked up a plate and put it in the sink. He washed it and stacked it on the draining board. Bubbles ran down and pooled in the grooves. He started on another plate.

A door slammed and someone shouted from behind the wall.

He fumbled with the plate, dropped it in the sink, and hot water splashed over his feet.

There was a bang, then voices. 'Why did you?' someone said. 'Why did you do it?' There was another bang, and a long silence.

Jay picked up the plate. It had cracked down the middle. He stroked the baby's cheeks. She seemed fine; she was pushing a bit of cracker around her tray, jabbing at it until it was wet and crumbly.

'Ham nu for,' she said, pointing to it.

'It's OK,' Jay told her. 'It's OK.'

He dried his hands, sat down, then got up and opened the door. He went outside and paced around the front of the houses. There were no cars; the house next door looked empty. In another house, further up the row, washing billowed on the line; trousers and shirts straining against their pegs as if they were trying to get away.

Something moved behind next door's window. Jay ran to the door and raised his hand to knock, his hand was in a fist, it was almost on the door, then he stopped and brought his hand down. He stood on the step for a long time.

The baby watched him. 'Wayha do int?' she said one morning. She looked at him carefully, as if she was waiting for an answer.

His wife got home late and they sat, almost asleep, on the sofa in front of the TV. Jay flicked through the channels – there were old programmes on that they used to watch, repeats that seemed half-familiar, the jokes coming in slightly different places than he remembered.

He put his arm round Lorna and she leaned her head back against him. He could see the freckle behind her ear. It was tiny, hardly more than a dot. He used to kiss her there.

She yawned and leaned in closer. Her hair was kinked from wearing headphones at work most of the day. Her eyes were dry and flecked with red.

The audience on the TV laughed raucously at something and he found the remote and turned it down.

He could hear her watch ticking. There was a phrase they used to say to each other when they'd first met – something about clocks or time, because she always used to be late, and he was about to say it to her, it used to make her laugh. But he couldn't remember it.

He'd seen her earlier on his phone and he'd grabbed it, almost yanked it out of her hands, but she was just checking a friend's number. His hand had been shaking and he'd gone upstairs so that she wouldn't notice.

He turned the volume up on the TV again and Lorna sighed and shifted her head so that it was against the cushion instead of his chest, and her hips moved, just slightly, away from his. His hand started to shake again, but it was nothing, he'd deleted everything, there had been no more phone calls. Any moment now she would turn back and lean against him again.

He was putting away the washing up – the cups and plates and glasses – in the cupboards and drawers. Everything was clean. Dinner was cooking. He was ahead for once. He lined the cups up carefully, and stacked the plates on top of each other. The glasses caught the light and gleamed.

A glass fell and smashed against the floor.

He reached up automatically to the shelf to stop any more falling but nothing had fallen, there was no broken glass anywhere.

There was another loud smash from behind the wall.

He put his hands over his ears and waited for it to stop.

~

The dishes were moving. If he hadn't been watching them every day, he might not have noticed, but he did watch them every day, and he saw them move. Soon they would be pointing straight in at the kitchen window.

~

The van was there again. He hadn't heard it drive up, or any doors opening and closing. But it was there. Jay watched it out of the window. He checked on the baby. He went back to the window, waited a moment, then went outside. He walked over to the van and looked in. There was an empty plastic bottle

46

under the seat, and a newspaper on the dashboard from a week earlier.

He circled the van twice in the drizzle, then thought about the number plate. What he should do was write down the number plate. He ran inside and found a pen, then crouched down next to the van to write. The number plate was covered in mud and he rubbed at it, saw an X and a 7, then rubbed again but the mud was too thick and wouldn't come off.

When he looked up, there was a light in one of next door's windows. It flicked on, then off. The curtains upstairs moved.

He walked over to the house. He glanced back at the road, then went closer, right up to the window. The rooms downstairs were dark. He pressed his ear against the glass but couldn't hear anything. Something moved further back in the house – maybe it was an arm, or someone's back, he just glimpsed something crossing into another room.

He ran round the side of his house, down the alley and through the long grass on the bank. He scrabbled over the brambles, dropped the pen, and scratched his hand on a broken bit of fence. There was a low wall behind the house next door. He jumped down softly. The back door was padlocked. The windows were shut and dark.

He stayed crouched against the concrete. The net curtains swayed against the glass.

Something rustled in the bank above him. The rustling got louder, and then a blackbird ran out towards him, scolding loudly.

He moved closer to the windows. They were smeared and dusty but he was sure there was something back there, in the darkness. He went closer. A voice murmured and someone laughed.

There was a shout behind him. He turned quickly. It was the farmer he'd seen in the field. She was walking towards him, calling out, asking what he was doing. He looked at her, then back at the window. He realised his hand was on the latch. His fingers were rigid and scratched, the nails bitten right down. It didn't look like his hand. He turned and ran, disappearing into his own house.

~

He jumped at small noises. When the baby broke her bowl he brushed up every single piece with the dustpan. He picked out the tiny shards from the cracks between the tiles.

It turned very cold. He stayed up late into the night with his ear to the kitchen wall, just the blue light from the fridge, and the white security lights coming in through the thin curtains. He paced the kitchen. When the baby cried he went straight to her and lifted her out of her cot and held her while he paced. She shaped her mouth into a sound and then gave up and blew a sticky bubble instead, and sighed.

'It's OK,' he told her. 'It's OK.'

Then he went back to the wall and listened. He pressed so hard that bits of paint flaked off onto the floor.

He left Lorna sleeping in bed and came downstairs and listened all night.

He heard the music again, faintly this time, somewhere towards the back of the house.

Another time there was a hushed, crying sound, like someone had left a tap slowly running.

~

'I no, I no,' the baby said. She opened her eyes wide. 'Sshhh,' she said.

~

The phone next door rang, cut out, then rang again. Jay stopped turning his phone on. He put it under a box in the wardrobe, then in a drawer. After a few days he took it out and threw it into the brambles behind the back window.

~

Someone was leaving. He heard it clearly and distinctly.

The baby looked at him, her head to one side. 'Wha?' she said. She frowned.

A very cold feeling washed over Jay – it went from his neck down to his feet, almost rooting him to the floor.

The voice came again through the wall. It was a man's voice, but not as deep as the one he usually heard. 'Going,' it said. 'The only thing to …' A cupboard opened, then drawers opened, and something heavy was dragged across the floor. A zip crunched.

Jay picked up the baby and held her to his chest. He stood by the front door. Footsteps thudded through the wall, more cupboards creaked open.

He put the baby in her coat, then went outside. He crossed the front yard. The van wasn't there. It was cold and the dishes seemed poised, tensed. They were pointing straight at him.

His breathing was fast and shallow. He held the baby tight and she pressed into his neck. 'Da?' she said.

There was no sound except for a rook cawing from a wet branch.

The house next door was in front of him. The door was half-open. Jay walked over to it slowly. He went up the step.

The rubble was still there. It was wet and bits of plaster had spread over the ground like snow. He pushed the door slowly and it swung inwards. It was quiet in there. There were no shoes by the door, no coats on the hooks. The hallway was long and dark. He turned and looked back towards where Lorna would be working. He imagined her at a desk, by a computer, listening.

He thought of how he would tell her.

He suddenly remembered the phrase they used to say to each other.

The phone rang. He held the baby tight. He took a deep breath and stepped inside.

Dreckly

Tide: 7.5 metres

What I'm about to tell you is the stupidest thing I've ever done. There was this one time when I bet Jory he couldn't swim out to that rock with all the seagull shit on it and of course he went right ahead and did it and I lost my entire savings which weren't really anything in the first place but still. I should have made sure the bet was for swimming out and back again because I had to call the coastguard for him on the way back, but there's no time to go into that now. And this other time I wanted to pierce my ears but they were charging way too much at the hairdresser's so I did it myself using an ice cube and a needle and a bottle of gin, and look how that turned out. I won't even tell you about that time with Leon – remember him? I can hardly even think about it. If I even just glimpse a gold tooth now I get this deep-down shudder – less like I've walked over my own grave than I've fallen right down into it. But now there's this, and this is probably worse.

It was me and it was Freya and it was Jory. We'd picked up the metal detectors and we were driving in my van to the beach. I was living in the van at that time, but that's another story. I had my shoes in the footwells, my toothbrush in the glove compartment, and dresses hanging across the windows for curtains. I'd strung up all these air-freshener things that looked like baubles, but it turned out all they did was make everything smell like a toilet at a festival.

Freya was sitting on the mattress in the back and she slid every time we cornered. Her dog, Mercury, kept whining and pawing at my pillow, right in the dent where my face went. Mercury's a greyhound that Freya found sleeping in a wheel-barrow somewhere. Freya can't ever leave anything if she finds it. Once there was a pigeon with a broken leg and after that no one saw her for weeks. She made a splint for it out of a cocktail stick. The thing about Mercury, though, is that she's really uptight. She'll stand completely still for hours, with just a single muscle quivering in her jaw, then suddenly, for no reason at all, she'll bolt and disappear. One of her eyes is milky blue, like a planet or something, but one of those planets that's completely screwed itself up and imploded.

'Hey look,' Freya said.

'I'm driving,' I told her.

'Hey look,' Freya said.

I turned around. She'd got a pair of my pants from God knows where and put them on Mercury's head. Mercury was walking backwards over the mattress and trying to shake them off. I didn't even know dogs could walk backwards.

'Get them off her you stupid bint,' I said.

Freya didn't move. She just sat there watching Mercury with that dopey expression she gets – as if the dog was her kid performing Shakespeare. The van bounced over a pothole and she had to duck her head to stop it hitting the roof. She's been six foot since we were about nine and then just got wider, like one of those giant redwoods. Whenever she goes in the supermarket someone always asks if she'll get something down for them from a high shelf – if she's in the right mood she does it, if she isn't she'll pass them something like absinthe or itch-relief cream and then walk away.

Jory finally turned around from the front seat and looked at what was going on. He's always about five minutes behind everyone else. I think it's because he's thinking about things but who can tell. He once found a body that had washed in and got caught amongst all these rock pools and it took him about an hour to realise it wasn't just someone sleeping. If you ask him why he thought someone was sleeping all twisted up in a rock pool he'll just shrug and say it was quiet down there. He likes quiet places where no one else goes. He took me out in his boat once and we just drifted for a long time.

I turned at the crossroads and the sea spread out in front of us. The beach down there is long and wide and packed every summer. We never go there in the summer. But now the holidays were over, and it was empty again, and we were doing what we always did after everyone had gone back home: scouring around with our metal detectors for whatever had been left behind. Sometimes we found money, jewellery, watches, and unopened cans of beer. But mostly we found belt buckles, keys, forks, tins smothered in barnacles. One time I found a bra and another time I found a crutch – I can understand forgetting a bra but I sometimes wonder how the person with the crutch got off the beach without noticing they'd left something important behind.

We borrow the metal detectors off Mr Warner. His son, Buddy, used to hang around with us before he moved away. Buddy had one of those BB guns and he once shot Jory in the leg with it. Jory won't tell anyone what it was about. Freya heard Buddy had made it out to Alaska and was working on boats – he and Jory had always wanted to work on boats – but I heard he'd married some crazy woman and had five kids in a caravan somewhere. Mr Warner told us he was working in insurance upcountry, which I guess is about in between.

The thing is, there used to be a whole load of us that came down to the beach and went around with the metal detectors. But, one by one, they all moved away and now we were the only ones left, doing the same old things over and over. We'd be twenty-six soon, then we'd be almost thirty. I didn't want to do it this year, and I sure as hell didn't want to be back doing it again next year – digging up tins and rusty coins, the three of us stuck up to our knees in the damp sand.

Tide: 7.0 metres

I parked next to the steps and we got out and looked down across the beach. There was no one around. There were brambles and sloe thickets all over the cliffs and Freya picked a blackberry, ate it, then spat it back out. She did the same thing every year – the blackberries up there are always sour, she just forgets every time.

The tide was high, a lot higher than usual, just like they'd told me at the pub the night before. I'd been in there with Jake and Lyn and Ricky and the talk had got around to how there was going to be this huge tide. It would come right up the beach, and then, when it dropped out, it would be so low that it would be possible to get round to the cove. Usually no one can get round to the cove but this time all the rocks leading over to it would be uncovered. And according to Lyn, who'd heard it from Morrie, who'd heard it from someone who'd seen it from their boat, all the sand and shingle had been scraped away by the spring storms.

'So you know what that means,' Lyn had said, leaning back on her stool until the legs looked like they were about to snap.

'Exactly,' Jake said, nodding slowly.

'Exactly,' Ricky said.

Then they all looked at me.

I knew what they were trying to do. Everyone knows about the cache that's supposed to be buried in the cove and how impossible it is to even get round there, let alone find it. They were trying to rile me up. They love getting me riled up. They'd done it before with the lottery ticket, and when the hospital was opened by that prince, and I wasn't going to give them the satisfaction this time.

So I just shrugged and didn't say a word. After a while I asked Ricky about his mother – she has this thing where she woke up one morning speaking French, even though she'd never spoken it before in her life – and then, when I thought I'd left it long enough, I finished my drink, stretched and got up. 'I guess I better head off,' I said.

'Early start in the morning then?' Lyn said, and they all practically stopped breathing from laughing, the bastards. That's the thing – people get certain ideas in their heads about you, and they never let you forget them. After a while, you find yourself doing exactly what they expect because mostly it's just easier.

I leaned into the van and got out the metal detectors and passed them round. Buddy's dad has a whole collection of them – most of them are old and a bit knackered; the kind with rusty coils rather than digital screens. He collects clocks too – they all chime on the hour across the house, slightly out of sync, and all these cuckoos and other weird crap jump out. I stayed over there once and I swear I still sometimes hear the ticking of each passing second.

'I've got the buggered one,' Freya said. She turned her detector over and examined it. 'Remember last year, there was one that kept whining? It just whined the whole time without stopping. I think I've got that one.'

'It's not doing it now,' Jory said.

'That's because I haven't turned it on yet dumb-ass.'

I locked up the van and put the key on a chain around my neck. I wasn't about to lose it like I did that other time, which wasn't even my fault, it was that bloody scarecrow in that bloody field, but that's another story.

'The tide's really high today,' I said.

'Turn it on then,' Jory said to Freya.

'It's going to go out really far,' I said.

'I'm trying to turn it on,' Freya said.

'We'd be able to get round to the cove.'

Freya kicked her metal detector and it made a screeching noise. She kicked it again and it stopped. 'Why would we want to do that?' she said.

I told them what everyone had been saying in the pub. 'Ricky was there,' I said. 'And Jake. They said Morrie said he'd heard it from someone on a boat.'

Freya broke off a bit of stick from the hedge and threw it for Mercury. Mercury didn't move. She pulled a long bit of ivy out and draped it around Mercury's neck.

'Cache,' she said. 'What the hell is a cache?'

'A hoard,' I said.

'A hoard?'

'Treasure for fuck's sake.'

Jory did up his rucksack and put it on his back. 'It's supposed to be drugs,' he said. 'From South America.' He always carries a rucksack. No one knows what he keeps in it.

'Ricky was being a total moron the other night,' Freya said. 'Did you see him doing that thing with the snooker cue?'

'Or gold coins,' Jory said. 'Bullion.'

'We just need to wait for the tide to drop,' I said.

'He's going to get kicked out soon,' Freya said. 'And then where will he go every night?' She opened a bottle and started walking down the steps to the beach.

'They let him back in before,' Jory said. He followed Freya down the steps. Mercury watched them, then suddenly ran, skidding down the loose stones.

I waited at the top for a minute, watching the tide. A few rocks had already started to appear. The water looked thick and creased, like oil. There was a container ship on the horizon. The sand was wide and empty. Sometimes, when I see the sand and rocks all bare like that, it looks like a building site: all brown and heaped up like it's going to become something else, but it never does, does it.

Tide: 5.8 metres

Freya and Jory started going over the beach from right to left, their detectors making those low, steady beeps that remind me of monitors in a hospital.

After a while Freya's detector started to beep faster and she stopped and moved it around until it became a single, high-pitched note. Jory opened his bag, got out a plastic kids' spade and started digging.

'It sounds like something big,' Freya said.

Jory kept digging. His hair blew around in the wind. There are streaks in there that look almost red – you know when the light catches that sandstone in the cliff? Not the crappy, claggy bits, the other stuff. But I don't know why I'm telling you that anyway.

'It's going to be big,' Freya said.

Jory dug some more, then reached in and pulled something out of the sand. It was a screwed-up bit of foil.

'Treasure,' Freya said. 'We've struck frigging foil.' She slapped me on the back and shook my hand. I slapped her back, harder. She took the foil from Jory and threw it for Mercury to chase, but Mercury was staring down at the sand and didn't even notice. Jory picked it up and put it in his pocket. He hates litter.

'We never find anything good,' I said.

'We found that bracelet last year,' Freya said. 'We sold it to Lyn.'

'It made her wrist go green.'

'Yeah but that's not our problem,' Freya said. She took another drink and passed the bottle round.

I turned and watched the tide. I could almost see it falling back, millimetre by millimetre. One minute there was a wrinkle in the water, the next it was the top of a rock. The first line of rocks had already appeared, wet and dripping, in front of us.

'If we find it we could do something,' I said.

'We are doing something,' Freya said.

'Something else.'

I scuffed my foot in the sand. Something else. Don't ask me what, exactly – all I know is that for years now Freya has been scrabbling around for shifts at the restaurant, only getting a few a week because her boss can pay all the younger people less. Once it's winter, her shifts will halve again and she'll be back to living off rice – all she eats is rice through the winter even though I told her I read somewhere that it's laced with arsenic. And then there's Jory, doing whatever the hell he always does – going for day-long walks on his own, doing up his boat, sleeping on Jake's floor which is the floor of a shed at the bottom of his dad's garden. They've dragged an old gas stove in there, which is probably going to blow up. I can smell gas as soon as I walk in but apparently, like with the arsenic, I'm just being paranoid. And then there's me, working in the same old hotel which is about to go under at any minute, serving the same old breakfasts of one stingy piece of bacon and mushrooms swimming in their own grey liquor, seeing things go on that would make your eyes water. Did I ever tell you about the thing with the machete? Remind me later.

Jory's detector started making a noise. It got louder, then softer, then it stopped.

'I heard Letty finally made it into acting,' Freya said.

'She was wooden,' I said. 'Remember that play we did at school?'

'She's got in some advert.'

'Toothpaste,' Jory said.

'Furniture,' I said, but it wasn't even funny.

'She's living with Mylo.'

'Mylo,' Jory said. 'What's she doing that for?'

'I heard he's manager of some hotel chain.'

'Which one?'

'We need to start going round in a minute,' I told them.

'The one with those beds in them.'

'They've all got beds in them,' I practically shouted. 'We've got to start in a minute, OK?' We had to time it exactly right, so that we'd have long enough to get round and back again before the tide came in and cut us off.

'There's loads of stuff here,' Freya said. She swept her detector over my shoes and it started beeping. What was supposed to happen was that I would take off my shoes and throw them at her, then she'd get the spade and dig at my feet, then I would trip her up and throw sand, and then she'd chase me even though she knows she'll never be able to catch me. When she starts doing it I just kind of have to go along with it. It's like when we order Chinese food and we share crispy beef – I don't even like crispy beef any more, but I don't exactly know how to tell her.

I took a step back, and then another. 'We've got to start going round,' I said.

Jory's detector beeped again. Freya stood there for a moment, watching me walk towards the rocks. I thought she was going to chase me and try to take my shoes, but she just watched me, a small frown on her face, then she bent down and started to dig.

I kept going. When I glanced back they'd got whatever it was out of the sand. It looked like someone's bent and rusty retainer. I knew that any minute now they would do that thing where they pretend the detector is a microphone, and Freya would hold up the retainer, lean right in, and pretend to be the first person she thought of with big teeth.

I got down to the rocks and started climbing.

Freya belted out a bar of June Carter.

Tide: 4.0 metres

The rocks were dark and slick with seaweed. My thighs scraped against mussels, which shone like wet lumps of coal. A gull banged at a limpet with its beak while I slipped and scraped, and slipped all over again, trying to keep hold of the bloody metal detector with one hand, and using the other to grip with. The beach already looked very far away.

I tried humming that crazy tune that always gets stuck in my head – you know how things always get stuck in my head, don't you – but all I kept doing was going over and over all the times I've tried to get out of here. I've tried a lot of things, if you want to know. I had this idea once, for example, that I would do up an old bus and go around selling food at campsites and festivals – everyone knows that people want to eat about a tonne of food when they've had too much to drink. Freya is like a hog at a trough when she's had a few, I can tell you, and probably I am too.

No one thought I would even get the bus, let alone the right paperwork for Chrissake, but I did, even though trying to memorise different types of bacteria for the hygiene certificate was one of the low points of my life. Have you heard of listeria?

That one's a complete bastard because it can grow even if the food's in the fridge.

I got Freya and Jory to come and help me at the first place; I paid them actually, and we got everything set up the night before, ready for breakfast the next morning. Then Freya got us these drinks and I swear I don't know what was in them, but I don't remember anything after that except being on Freya's shoulders with this ukulele band playing next to us, and a lot of lights flashing, and Jory, Jory was definitely there, very close. We didn't make any food the whole weekend.

Then I thought I would train as a lifeguard, because those lifeguards go everywhere, don't they. I figured I'd better practise first though because it'd been a while since I'd been in the sea and I don't really like it that much to be honest – all that stuff brushing past your legs, and stones bruising your feet, and have you ever been in when you know the kid next to you is peeing? I hate that; their innocent face, the slightly strained look around their eyes. I don't know about you but I probably wouldn't save a kid if I knew it had just pissed through its wetsuit.

So I got Freya to paddle out and pretend to drown so that I could rescue her, only it turns out that the stupid bint can't actually swim. Somehow she forgot to tell me that piece of information. She started flailing around, and I thought she was just pretending really well until she panicked and clung onto my neck and dragged me under. We came up gasping then went under again. I don't actually remember how we got out, but somehow, finally, we were lying on the sand and Freya was coughing and I was coughing and we were pummelling each other's backs for a lot longer than we probably needed to.

After that I sort of lost interest in the whole idea.

There are about a million other things I've tried as well, but I don't feel like going into them now. I even started drawing this book for kids, about a man who forgets where he lives and just wanders around from door to door, knocking. Sometimes people let him in but mostly they don't. It took ages and then I showed it to Jory and he looked at it for a long time, just sitting there, turning the pages slowly without saying anything. He never said anything at all.

Tide: 2.5 metres

There was this clattering noise and Mercury ran straight past me over the rocks, almost ramming into my legs. The gull lifted upwards, screaming. Freya's voice came over on the wind, I couldn't hear what she said, but I turned round and they were both climbing over the rocks behind me.

I stopped and waited. The tide was very low now. All I could see in either direction were wide, flat rocks, like shelves, and rock pools in between them. There were rock pools everywhere – some were shallow, some were smaller than my hand, others were so narrow and deep that I couldn't see the bottom. They smelled leafy, sort of vegetable, and they were full of this bright red and green weed. I kept glimpsing things darting around, but whatever they were they always disappeared before I could properly look, leaving the water rippling. There's a programme

I saw on TV once about rock pools; how, every moment, something is trying to kill something else: limpets crushing barnacles, anemones rasping bits off other anemones, starfish cracking open mussels like walnuts. But on the surface they look so still.

Jory stepped quickly from rock to rock, like some kind of pro. He was carrying his metal detector in one hand, his other hand was in his pocket, and Freya's bottle clinked in his ruck-sack. Freya didn't have her metal detector any more. She was down on all fours, making low, grumbling sounds.

'I'm getting cramp,' she said. 'I can feel it in my leg.'

'We're almost there,' I told her, which was a lie because I couldn't even see the cove yet. Those rocks went on for ever; they were so bony and ridged it was like being on the moon or something.

'I'm hungry,' Freya said. 'God I am so hungry.'

'We need to get round quicker than this,' I said.

'I need salt. That's why my leg's cramping. I need salt.'

'Stop thinking about it,' I told her. Freya's cramps are the bane of my entire life. One time there was this guy at a party and let's just say things were progressing, and then Freya came up, almost bent over with pain. I asked her what the matter was, thinking it was something really bad, and she said it was cramp in her little toe. She couldn't walk or do anything. She took herself off into a corner like some animal nobly going off to die, and I ended up having to bend her toe back for over an hour until it eased, and the guy went off with someone else.

Freya stopped crawling and sat down.

'We don't have any salt,' I said. 'Get up.'

Jory kept walking, thank God, but a second later he stopped. He pointed at a clump of seaweed. 'You can eat that,' he said.

Freya looked at it. 'You serious?' she said.

'We don't have time for this,' I told her.

'That one's nice,' Jory said. 'Salty.'

'Jesus Christ,' I said.

Freya went over and picked up a handful of dark green strands. She raised them up to her mouth.

'Wait,' Jory said suddenly. 'Don't eat it.'

Freya dropped the seaweed and spat on the rocks. She kept spitting even though she hadn't eaten any of it. 'You're a frigging fiend,' she said. 'You told me I could eat it.'

Jory pointed at a trickle of yellow on the rock. 'I think Mercury got there first.'

I started clambering again. This time I didn't wait to see if they were following. If I'd waited, we'd have been stuck on those rocks until the tide covered us slowly over.

Tide: 1.2 metres

After a while Jory caught up with me. I could hear Freya somewhere far behind, crawling along next to Mercury, complaining to her, and Mercury making these small yippy replies, complaining right back.

I watched Jory as he moved. He never slipped. I was watching him quite a lot and then there was a trench between two rocks and my foot went down into it. He came over and pulled me back up. His hand was cool and slightly rough. I got this sudden memory of him from when we were younger. He was in the playground looking at the bark chips under the swing, and he reached down, picked one up, and ate it. He chewed on it for a long time with his eyes closed, as if there was no one else around him. I actually get that memory quite a lot. I wonder what he'd think if he knew I'd watched him, and that I remembered it almost every time I saw him.

I looked over towards the cove. 'What if we find it?' I said.

Jory was looking at the cliffs. 'There are supposed to be fossils round here.'

'It's meant to be right over there,' I said. 'Just waiting, under the sand.'

'They're like ferns,' Jory said. 'We could look for them some-time, if you want.'

'What will Lyn say if I find it?' I said. The edge of the cove was up ahead. I'd only ever seen it from the top of the cliff before. It looked wider from here and it was covered in bits of thin, slatey rock, as if a roof had slid down and smashed. A few more minutes and we'd be there.

My hand started to feel very hot. I looked down and realised I was still holding Jory's hand.

Jory looked down too but he didn't move. My hand was so hot it was almost burning.

'The tide's going to turn soon,' I said.

Jory nodded. His hand slipped away. He jumped over a rock and I followed.

'I liked that bit in your drawings,' he said, 'where the man knows it's about to get dark, but he decides to try one more door.'

I stopped. 'You remember that?' I said.

A crow glided down and landed on top of a rock. It watched us carefully.

Jory reached across and helped me over another gulley and suddenly we were there, on the gritty sand in the cove.

Tide: 0.5 metres

No one had been there for a long time. I know the tide comes in and washes everyone's footprints away so it's not like you can ever really tell, but it felt like no one had been on that beach for a really long time. There was a sort of hush to it. I could hear every loose stone that rolled.

I called to Freya to hurry up, then I switched my metal detector on and started going up the beach towards the cliffs.

'Wait a second,' Freya shouted. 'Mercury's seen something.' I turned round and Mercury was staring down past the rocks towards the water. Even her tail was tense.

'Come on,' I said.

'I think there's a bird down there,' Jory said.

'She's about to go,' Freya said. 'Look at her.'

'It might be a plover,' Jory said.

'Come on,' I said again, but I knew they weren't going to. They were never going to. Bloody Jory with his seaweed and his birds and his boat. Bloody Freya, clinging on to my neck and dragging me under. I turned away and walked faster up the beach.

The slates crunched under my shoes. I went past heaps of rope and wood and plastic boxes that had been stranded by the tide. There were little flies jumping all over them. The seaweed looked baked and brittle.

Behind me, Mercury let out a low, strangled bark, Freya shouted something, and there was the sound of feet against stones. When I looked back, the three of them were no more than specks on the wet sand at the edge of the water.

I moved my detector in slow wide arcs. It made no sound, not even the smallest beep.

Tide: 1.1 metres

I started walking in zigzags to cover more ground, swinging the metal detector from one side to the other. I went up a stony slope and then across a series of slates that cracked under my feet. I went back down the slope. I climbed over a pile of wooden boards and pushed the detector right under them, but still there was nothing.

I moved across the back of the cove, so that I was right at the base of the cliffs. The stones and shingle had all been churned up, just like they'd told me. A whole layer of stones had been scraped off, and underneath the sand looked raw and pale.

I went right over that sand, every millimetre of it. At one point my detector let out a faint whine and I stopped, bent down and dug with my hand around the stones, but all I found was a sweet wrapper. I dropped it and kept going. I went back the way I'd come, working backwards and forwards over the same area. I must have missed something, I must have. I checked my metal detector, running it over the tops of my shoes. It let out a long, wavering beep.

I turned and looked down at the water. The lowest line of rocks had already been covered back over. I ran to the next bit of sand, and then the next.

Something moved behind me and I think I must have swung the metal detector round because there was a yelp and then I saw it was Mercury, standing right next to my legs.

'Shit, you stupid hound,' I said. 'What are you doing?'

She leaned into me and I stroked her bony head.

'Find it then,' I said. 'Find the cache.'

She looked at me like she didn't know what a cache was either.

'The treasure,' I said. 'Find the treasure, OK?'

She barked at me, then arched her back and sidled away, like a crab or something. Then she darted back and lunged at my shoes.

'Piss off,' I said.

She darted backwards, then lunged again. I skipped my feet out of the way.

'Piss off Mercury,' I said.

I pushed the detector under a stone and moved it around. Then I pushed it under another one. Mercury lunged again. Bits of grit clattered quietly down the cliff.

I let her gnaw on my shoes until she got bored and ran away. I sat down and let the metal detector fall on the ground behind me. My legs were aching. My throat was parched. Bits of shingle dug into my thighs and arse.

I closed my eyes. When I opened them again I could see Freya and Jory messing around down in the shallows. They were pushing each other and suddenly Freya reared up and tipped Jory right in. I heard the splash from up the beach. He got up, flailing, and ran at her. She sidestepped somehow. They were both laughing their asses off and I was laughing too and I got up and started making my way down to them. I was going to push Freya in and then I was going to, well I didn't know what I was going to do to Jory.

That's when my detector started to beep. I stopped and looked back at it. I thought I'd probably knocked it on my way past. The noise was louder than usual, more insistent. 'What the hell are you doing?' I said. I kicked it but it didn't stop.

I looked back at the sea. My throat got even dryer. I crouched down and dug into the cold sand. My fingers touched something hard. I kept digging until I found an edge. I scraped the sand off and there was the corner of a metal box.

I stopped digging and looked up. Freya was waving her arms at me and Jory was wringing out his wet hair. The water was glinting off them and the light was this weird haze – I can't really describe it, but you know when light comes down through trees, it was kind of like that, and I know there were no trees, I'm not an idiot, but the beach was deserted, it was all empty and it was ours, the whole place was ours.

They started coming back up the beach and Jory called something but I couldn't hear what he said.

My hand was on the edge of the box.

Freya waved again. 'Next year,' she shouted. 'Next year, OK, dickhead?'

Next year. I ran my hands right around the edge. It was big. It felt heavy and wedged in. I started to prise it out.

What had I said to them? We could do something else. I thought of being on Freya's shoulders, and heaving her out of the water. I thought of the way I had drifted in Jory's boat.

I moved my hand and pushed a heap of sand forwards. Then I did it again, pushing with both hands. I kept pushing the sand until the box was buried. I covered it right over and stamped down around it. When I looked up Mercury was back. She was just standing there, watching me. We stared at each other for a moment, then I got up and ran down to the rocks.

'I was calling you for ages,' Freya said.

I brushed the sand off my hands. It was so sharp and gritty it had left scratches in my nails.

'What's the matter with you?' Freya said. 'You look weird.'

Jory looked at me closely. He smelled like sweat and the sea. 'It was a good idea,' he said. 'Coming over here.'

'You almost made me eat piss,' Freya said.

We went back across the rocks. The sea came in and covered them over, millimetre by millimetre, and all the time it glittered like coins.

Mercury kept turning round to look at me and I had this feeling that she'd seen the box, that she knew, and would look at me differently now with her wild blue eye.

We got back to the beach. We got in the van. We drove away.

And that's it. That's all I really have to tell you. I suppose you'll want to know that I went back. It was a few days later and I waited until low tide and tried to get round but it wasn't low enough and halfway there I had to turn back, water lapping at my ankles.

I suppose you'll want to know that I didn't tell Lyn or Ricky or Jake anything about it. And that, after the autumn storms, in reference to another conversation entirely, they said that the sand and the stones in the cove had heaped up and shifted around and that it all looked completely different again.

I suppose you'll want to know that last night I ate crispy titting beef.

And I suppose you'll want to know why I did it. What am I supposed to tell you? Sometimes you feel like opening something up and sometimes you don't. And that's all I have to say about it, OK.

One Foot in Front
of the Other

SHE WALKS DOWN THE track and climbs the first gate. Her legs ache. They are heavy as wet bales. She's been walking for a long time, although she can't remember how long exactly. Her jeans are soaked to the knees; there's a bramble hooked on the back of her shirt and another around her foot. Her grey hair is damp, brittle, and there's a moth caught in it. There's a scratch along the bottom of her jaw.

She climbs the first gate. She's been walking for a long time. She doesn't have anything with her unless you count the brambles or the moth. She walks over the field, which is bare and dewy. The barley has just been cut back to stubble. It's early and the air is wet – damp gusts blow in like smoke before the fire's got going properly. It will be hot later; the sun will break through and parch everything. She walks faster. A gunshot goes off in the distance. All she wants to do is get back. There is the constant sound of hammering from somewhere, and chain-saws, and the terrible screech of an angle grinder.

She crosses the field and comes to the next gate. There are cows standing on the other side of it. She stops for a moment in the churned, hoofy mud. The tree next to her is bent at the hips, staring at the ground. There's a line of ants down there, carrying a green dragonfly. She goes over to the gate and climbs the first rung. The cows huddle together and press against the bars. They are a dark brown mass. She claps her hands but they don't move. She rattles the gate but they don't move. She climbs down. The cows' skin twitches, as if something has run over it.

She crosses the field and goes into the next one. There is the constant sound of hammering from somewhere. The gate is in the far corner and she walks over to it. A gunshot goes off in the distance. There is a drinking trough in front of the gate. She's suddenly thirsty. It feels like a long time since she's eaten or had a drink of anything. She goes over to the trough and dips her hands in. The water is dark and cold. There are flies stuck on the creased surface. She dips her hands in and cups some water and splashes it over her face and down her throat. The water is so cold she almost can't feel it. She splashes some more. Her hands and throat are numb. She still feels thirsty.

When she looks up there's a herd in front of her, pressing against the other side of the gate. They are pressed silently, tensely, as if they are waiting for something. She doesn't know if they're the same cows or not. They are a dark brown mass. A cow leans its head over the top bar and rubs its jaw along the metal. One eye watches her while the other rolls.

'What are you doing?' she says. 'Get away.' She climbs the gate and bangs her hands on the bar. The cows don't move. Their breath comes in thick shapes on the air.

She waits a moment. All she wants to do is get back. She's been walking a long time and her legs ache. But the cows still don't move. Only their tails flick. She turns and looks back at the way she's come. There is a chainsaw somewhere, and the terrible screech of an angle grinder. The gates through the fields are the quickest way of crossing down, she remembers that much, even though she hasn't been back for a long time. Otherwise she'd have to loop right up to the main road, hike along for a few miles, then come down that way. She doesn't want to go up to the main road. What she needs to do is cross the fields, get onto the lane, aim for the slope, then cut across the trees from there.

She follows the edge of the field until she finds a gap in the hedge. She pushes through it. Brambles catch at her clothes. The sleeve of her shirt tears. She gets a scratch across the wrist. Finally she is out and in the lane. The lane is narrow and stony. The nettles on the banks are taller than her and there's cow parsley with stems as thick as fingers. She keeps going. Her legs ache and her hair is damp. The potholes are filled with oily water. A jackdaw is splayed on the ground.

There's a low noise ahead but she keeps going. The nettles thicken on either side until she's brushing past them with both shoulders. Flies knock into her. The nettles lean. There's a sort of clopping noise coming from somewhere. A gunshot goes off in the distance. The lane dips downwards. She turns a corner and the cows are coming up the lane in front of her, three abreast, walking slowly and looking straight at her.

She raises her arms. 'Get away,' she says. 'Get away.'

The cows come forwards slowly. They're pressed into each other, their flanks are rasping, and the cows at each edge push into the nettles, bending and trampling them.

She waves her arms. They don't stop. She stamps her feet and shouts but they keep coming. She turns and walks back to the hedge and goes along it, looking for the gap. The cows are closer now. She walks quickly along the hedge. There's no gap. The cows are right behind her. They're walking slowly and steadily. She pushes her hands into the hedge. It's too thick to get through. She pushes again. Something cuts her hand. A nettle loops over her foot. She pushes harder. There's the gap. She stumbles in and crouches on the ground. The cows walk carefully, pressing into the hedge. When they reach the gap they slow down and then stop. They smell of old grass and dry skin and the sticky mud around their feet. They stand in the lane and shift their weight from side to side. She stays crouched. Her legs ache. There is a small bone and some fur on the ground by her foot. Whenever she moves the cows' skin twitches.

She backs out of the hedge and into the field on the other side. She looks once more through the gap. The cows snort. One of them stamps. She walks back through the empty field. There's only one way left to go – over to the main road and across from there. All she wants to do is get back. She can't remember how long she's been walking. It must be a long time.

There is the constant sound of hammering from somewhere. She crosses the first field and enters the second. A gunshot goes off in the distance. This field has long wet grass that sticks to her legs. It tangles in clumps and trips her up. It's tough and doesn't snap across her boots. She keeps going. There isn't far to go. She can't remember exactly, but surely there isn't far to go.

The next field is wide and open and more land, more fields, stretch in front of her, strung with telegraph poles and bending trees. The road is in the distance – it thrums with tractors and brewery lorries and lorries delivering frozen food. They flash on the horizon – red, blue, red, blue. They seem very far away.

The gate she needs is ahead, in the opposite corner of the field. There is the sound of a chainsaw somewhere. She starts to cross the field. As soon as she starts crossing, she sees the cows. They are on the far side, walking towards the gate. She walks faster. The cows seem to quicken their pace. She keeps walking. The cows will reach the gate first, she knows it, they are closer than she is. She walks faster. The cows are in a line, now they are in a group, pushing against each other. Her legs ache. She doesn't want to run but she starts running. The cows start running.

All she sees is the gate. The cows' hooves strike at the ground. A gunshot goes off in the distance. The cows' bodies send out a wave of heat and it is behind her as she runs. She stumbles in the mud. Her foot sticks. She gets to the gate. Her foot is on the rung. She slips. A cow thuds against the gate and it shakes on its hinges. She slips again, then she is up and over and on the other side.

She doesn't turn around until she's almost across the field. All she wants to do is get back. Then she makes herself turn. The cows have gone. The fields are empty all around her. Below there is a dark line of trees. She hobbles down, mud on her legs, grass on her legs, brambles hooked to the back of her shirt. A crow circles.

Her foot catches on a stone and she stumbles and almost falls. Her nose is raw and the numb feeling has spread up her hands and into her arms. The mist is pushing in thicker now, dropping down so that everything is swathed up to knee height. She can't see the ground, or her feet. Her feet are very cold. There is the constant sound of hammering from somewhere, and chainsaws, and the terrible screech of an angle grinder.

She makes her way down the slope and towards the trees. Once she is on the other side of the trees she will almost be back. There is a sound ahead of her and at first she thinks it must be her boots hitting the stones in the grass. She keeps going. The crow is still circling. A gunshot goes off in the distance.

The first cow comes up the slope towards her. There are two more behind it. They come in ones and twos, slowly, with their heads down, pushing closer. The whole herd is there, coming up the slope about twenty yards ahead, wading through the mist, and spreading out in a semicircle around her.

She stops. The fields are dark and empty for miles in all directions.

The cows don't run, they don't stamp, they just press slowly forwards.

She stays where she is. Her legs ache. She's been walking for a long time. She can't remember how long exactly. All she wants to do is get back. There is the constant sound of hammering from somewhere.

She takes a step backwards, and then another, until she's up the slope and across the field, one slow step at a time. The cows don't move. She doesn't take her eyes off them. Their tails flick. Their breath comes out in thick shapes on the air.

She reaches the gate. She climbs back over it. What she needs to do is circle around another way. She needs to go back to the first field and start again. She needs to climb the gate, and then the next one, and then she will be back. She hasn't been back for a long time – she can't remember how long, exactly.

She crosses into the first field. The nettles along the edges are taller than she is. She doesn't have anything with her unless you count the brambles or the moth in her hair. The field is bare and dewy. The barley has just been cut back to stubble. It will be very hot later; the sun will break through and parch everything. She walks faster. She sees the gate. There is the terrible sound of an angle grinder somewhere. Damp gusts blow in like smoke before the fire's got going properly.

Way the Hell Out

'DID YOU HEAR ABOUT the Ellis house,' Fran says. She picks up her mug, holds it, but doesn't take a drink.

'It's coming up for sale again,' Morrie says. He leans back and looks around the café. It's empty apart from a table of three people in the corner. He nods to them. 'Lyn,' he says. 'Jake. Ricky.'

They all nod back then carry on eating.

The owner of the café stands behind the counter, drying glasses and wrapping cutlery.

'That's because it's happened again,' Fran says.

Morrie nods and takes a drink. The windows drip with steam from the inside, rain from the outside.

Fran puts her mug back down on the table but keeps hold of the handle. 'It didn't start straight away,' she says. 'When they first moved in, everything was fine.'

'It's a nice old house,' Morrie says.

'They bought it for their holidays.'

'They paid a lot for it.'

'They wanted the quiet.'

'It's definitely quiet out there.'

'No other houses.'

'No lights.'

'No traffic on the road.'

'You wouldn't see anyone else for days.'

'Shut the door, light the fire, close up all the curtains.'

Morrie finishes his drink. 'I like a fire.'

'You'd need it out there, the way the wind comes in.'

'It does come in.'

'The sea mists.'

'They do come in.'

They both look out of the window. A sheet of rain presses against the glass. The group in the corner sit in silence. There's just the sound of their forks against their plates.

'It's a shame,' Fran says. 'The way it starts happening.'

Morrie leans back further in his chair. 'Same as before?'

Fran leans forward. 'Same as before. They come back and find the door's unlocked. At first they think they just forgot.'

'It's easy to forget.'

'But the next day it's unlocked again,' Fran says. 'So they lock everything carefully, check it over, and go to bed. In the morning, all the windows have been flung wide open.'

The café owner starts stacking the glasses on a shelf. Each glass grates against the next as he stacks them.

'They close all the windows and put the latches down. They check the doors. And for a few days nothing happens. They almost forget about it. The windows are so loose that maybe they just opened by themselves in the wind.'

Morrie nods again, slowly.

'Then one night they hear someone walking down the road.'

'No one walks down that road.'

'But they hear someone. Boots on the gravel. A cough. Whoever it is they're dragging their feet. They're unhurried.'

'It doesn't seem right,' Morrie says.

'They look out and try to see who it is. The road's empty. There's no one there.'

'What about in the trees?'

'That's next.' Fran twists her mug around and holds it with her other hand. 'They start thinking there's something in the trees.'

'What?'

'They can't tell – they have those thick pines out there, and at first it just looks like a dark shape, maybe a gap between branches.'

'Pine trees can do that.'

'Then they realise what it is.'

A glass falls off the shelf and cracks against the floor. No one jumps.

'It's a figure, just standing there, looking across at the house. It's standing very still. There's some kind of hood, maybe a long coat.'

Morrie sighs and shakes his head.

'It's dark, so they try to find a torch, but by the time they've found it there's nothing there, just the gaps between the trees.' Fran glances at the group at the other table. They've all got their heads down, eating. 'They try to tell themselves it was nothing. Just the wind, just the trees moving.'

'The wind does move things out there.'

'It does.'

A chair scrapes against the floor but no one gets up.

'They tell themselves they didn't really see anything. And for a while they don't see anything else. Everything goes back to how it was, until they come back one day and, as they're getting out of their car, they happen to look across at their kitchen window.' Fran stops again and looks down at her tea. There's half left but she still doesn't drink it. 'There's hands pressed against it, from the inside.'

'The inside?'

'Two hands, just pressing.'

'I don't like that,' Morrie says. 'That's not right.'

'After that they stay up all night. They check each room. They sit on the sofa and put the TV on loud. They try not to think about the hands.'

The cutlery clinks as the café owner wraps some more and puts it carefully in a basket.

'But they must fall asleep, because when they wake up, someone's in the room.'

'I don't like that,' Morrie says.

'There's someone behind them, near the door. It's dark and they've just woken up, and the figure is moving carefully, keeping close to the walls. It walks through the house, down the corridor and out of the front door.'

Someone on the other table knocks their plate with their elbow and it rocks, then slowly stills.

Morrie shakes his head. 'They only bought it for their holidays.'

'Not much of a holiday.'

'What did they do?'

'Same as the people before. They phoned the police.'

'There's no signal out there.'

'There's no anything out there.'

'They probably had to go to the top of the road to ring.'

'In the wind.'

'In the rain.'

They look out of the window. The café owner folds and wraps. The cutlery basket is almost full.

'Of course, by the time the police get there the house is empty again.'

'What did they say?'

'What could they say.'

'The doors are all locked.'

'No marks, no traces. No other witnesses. What can they do.'

'It is quiet out there.' Morrie watches a drop of water as it moves slowly down the window. 'I suppose they don't really know anyone.'

'I suppose not.'

'Out there on their own.'

Someone walks past the door and slows down. Everyone watches. The person stops, looks in, then carries on walking.

'They stop coming down so often.'

'No one they can talk to,' Morrie says. 'That's not right.'

'And when they do come back, things have been moved.'

'The rugs?'

'The books. Furniture.'

'The rugs?'

'Probably the rugs.'

'I don't like that,' Morrie says.

The door of the café rattles in the wind. The café owner crosses the room, looks out, then pulls it tightly shut.

'Eventually they stop coming down at all,' Fran says.

'That's what the others did.'

'That's what they always do.' She watches the café owner as he walks back behind the counter. 'They stop coming down and then they sell it.'

'They'll want to sell it quick.'

'They will.'

'It'll probably be a bargain.'

'No doubt.'

'Like last time.'

'No doubt.'

Fran turns and gets her coat off the back of her chair. She puts it on but stays sitting. She picks up her mug again. The group on the other table hold their forks but don't eat.

'Someone'll snap it up of course,' Fran says.

'Buy it cheap, sell it expensive,' Morrie says.

'That's what she always does.'

Fran finishes her drink in one mouthful. The café owner wraps the last of the cutlery and switches on the radio. The group on the other table start to talk amongst themselves.

'She's always been a swine, that Jane Ellis,' Fran says. She gets up and zips her coat.

Salthouse

WINTERS ARE WHEN PEOPLE disappear. One minute you're elbow to elbow on the street, the next you walk along side-stepping nothing but the wind. Cafés put down their blinds. Houses are locked and dark. The car parks slowly empty and all that's left on the beaches are a few forgotten shoes. Waiters and waitresses go away to work the ski season, cleaning chalets in a bright glare of snow. Lifeguards pack their tents and dented surfboards and get on planes, following the sun like a flock of migrating birds.

I wait for Gina by the door, my coat and trainers on, and the old, dried-up Christmas tree leaning against the wall. It's not even four o'clock, but the sky is already dim – one of those days where it never really gets light except for a pale streak above the sea. Gina lives a few streets away in a bungalow that's almost identical to mine, except hers has a hole in the wall from where her mother once tried to decorate and then gave up halfway through. There's a TV in front of it now but you can still see the cracked edges. It takes two minutes to walk between our houses; one and a half if you take the alley with the mattress and the bin bags. Down the sides of each street there's clumps of sea beet, burdock, grass that knots into sandy bouquets. The grass is sharp and tough. We used to take turns ripping out handfuls and seeing who would get cuts across their fingers. There's sand everywhere around here. When you walk in the wind, grains crunch against your teeth. We're out on the edge of town, where the cliffs start to crumble and turn to sloping dunes. The dunes are heavy and soft, like flour in a bowl. They never stay still. They slip and shift around; sometimes growing, sometimes flattening out. When the gales come, loose sand blows down the road and heaps at our front doors.

Gina finally knocks and I go straight out, dragging the tree behind me. 'I thought you were coming earlier,' I say. I prop the tree up and lock the door, then start hauling it down the steps. We always bury the tree together first thing in the new year, but somehow it's already halfway through February. The tree's almost bare, except for a few brown needles clinging on.

'You look like you're moving a body,' Gina says.

'I thought you were coming earlier,' I tell her.

Gina turns and looks back up the road, as if she's seen something, but there's nothing there. 'How late are your parents working tonight?'

'Late,' I say. The care home they manage is full and low on staff. 'Mr Richards is sleepwalking again. He's started getting out and trying to hitch-hike at the side of the road. No one's stopped for him yet.'

Gina picks up her end of the tree but doesn't move off the step. 'Late,' she says.

I start walking backwards, then turn and hold the tree behind me so that I can walk facing the right way. We cross the street and cut across a few front gardens. A cat follows us, then yawns and sits by somebody's door. We pass the last of the bungalows, with their banging shutters and wind-cracked paint, and come out onto the road. The dunes spread out ahead of us, humped and dark. We start down the road towards them. Every year we take our tree down to Salthouse and bury it along with everyone else's, to try and stop the sand moving and the dunes disappearing. There are rows and rows of old trees. Gina and I always find the best place, and dig ours in the deepest. We do it with my tree because Gina's is plastic and has flashing lights and a singing snowman on top.

The wind slaps into us. I pull up my hood and button it under my chin. I wait for Gina to do the same, then realise she isn't wearing her coat. She's had the same one since we were about seven – a parka with a broken zip and sand in the pockets, which used to come down past her knees. Once, we both fitted into it at the same time. Instead of her coat, she's wearing a white jumper that looks too small for her, and instead of trainers, she's wearing long brown boots that must be her mother's. They're too big for her. She keeps stopping to wedge her feet in tighter.

'Where's your coat?' I ask. I have a loose tooth and I keep touching it with my tongue. I've lost all the others – some have grown back, some are halfway through – and this is the only original tooth I have left. It should have come out weeks ago. Usually I would bend it until it makes a gristly, crackling noise, and twist it at the root, but with this tooth I push downwards, into the gum, until it settles back in place.

Another gust of wind hits us, and Gina rakes her hair out of her mouth. Her hair is very pale and so is her skin and the tips of her eyelashes, like grass that has dried in a heatwave. Her mouth is small and dark and she smells sweet and sour, like a vinegary strawberry I once ate and spat back out.

'You need to pull that tooth,' she says. 'I'll do it for you if you want.' I can feel her shivering – it goes down through the tree and into my hands.

We come to the crossroads and I start following the path down to the dunes, but Gina stops and puts her end of the tree down. She picks at a dry needle in her finger. By now our palms are stippled. The lights of town are in the distance. A bus goes past, its insides lit up like an aquarium. There is the sound of the wind, and the sound of the sea, and something I can't place, a low beating that isn't the wind or the sea.

'The fair's back,' Gina says.

I can just make out a small, hazy glow past the hotels. 'Remember the dodgems?' I say.

'You rammed that old woman until she almost got concussion.'

'She did it to me first.'

'They still have them,' she says. 'And they have this pendulum thing now, where you get tipped upside down.'

94

I watch her pick at her finger. 'You've been,' I say.

She gets the needle out and drops it. 'It's been here all week.' Again, she turns and looks down the road, at nothing.

The beat of the fair surges in, louder for a moment, on the back of the wind. I start dragging the tree towards the path.

'Evie,' Gina says.

'We need to get going with this.'

'Evie,' Gina says.

'We're almost there.'

'We could do the tree after.'

'It'll be too dark after.'

'We'll get covered in sand if we do it first.'

'It'll be too dark after,' I say.

'Remember that time you broke your parents' window, kicking that stone, and I told them it was me?' Gina says. 'Remember when I taught you how to go really hot and dizzy, so you look too ill for school?'

I keep my eyes on the ground and push at my tooth. If I look up that's it; especially with her reminding me of all the things I owe her like that.

'Remember when we were five and we found those flies on top of each other and we pulled off their wings, and afterwards you couldn't bear it, so I stuck them back on with superglue?'

I look up. 'It didn't work,' I say.

Gina picks up her end of the tree. She knows we're going. 'What didn't?'

'The glue,' I say. 'You told me they flew away but I found them later, on the windowsill.'

The beat of the fair gets louder as the road slopes into town. Every time the wind hits, the tree loses more needles. They scatter along the pavement like hair on the floor of a hairdresser's.

'Look at Mrs Bradley's house,' Gina says. 'She got another ornament.' She points to a hare by the front door. There are moths attached to the wall, and a few hunched gnomes on the grass. Mrs Bradley taught us for years, before we moved to secondary school last September. She showed us how to dissect a frog. All I remember are the thin, splayed-out hands, how they looked like they were asking for something. Behind her desk she had a shelf of jars with frogs' legs and fish and something small and twisted, all floating around in salty water. They looked like the pickle jars in Gina's mother's kitchen – gherkins, silverskins, shredded beetroot – and once Gina made us eat some and pretend we were eating whatever it was in Mrs Bradley's jars. I threw up first. One time, Mrs Bradley brought in a pair of calf's lungs and inflated them by blowing with a straw and one kid fainted and smacked his mouth on the wall and his two front teeth slid right out next to my shoes.

As we go past, Gina glances round, then climbs over the wall and puts the hare in the middle of the driveway. Then she moves a weird baby gnome so that it's nestled behind the front wheel of the car. We don't like babies and swore a long time ago that having them was nothing to do with us.

As we get closer the music thrums up the road and into my stomach. The fair's in a car park that belongs to a hotel that's been boarded up for as long as I can remember. There's a pile of beer cans at the entrance, and ticket stubs scattered over the ground. Lights throb like something painful. Someone lets out a long low howl. It's still only the afternoon but suddenly it feels dark and late. A kid runs past wearing a crash helmet, chasing a balloon that's been wrenched away by the wind.

We go through the gate, then Gina stops and I almost trip. I can see that she's trying to smooth down her hair and her clothes without me noticing.

'What are you doing?' I say.

'Do I look OK?'

There's sand on her boots and her hair has gone curly in the salty wind. Her cheeks are pink along the top of the bone. I haven't noticed those bones before. They make her face look narrower, as if a new one is slowly being chiselled out. How haven't I noticed them?

I put my hand up to my own face and feel the same soft, puckering skin that is already flushed and burning under the hot lights.

'OK for what?' I say. I say it stiffly, my mouth suddenly dry. I start backing in with the tree, but Gina doesn't move.

'We have to put this somewhere,' she says.

'We'll just hold it.'

'Put it under this van.'

'I'll hold it.'

'Just slide it under here.'

There are a group of vans with the fair's logo on parked near the wall. Gina crouches down and slides the tree under one of them. 'We'll come and get it later,' she says. 'OK?'

She doesn't wait for me to answer. I turn back one more time to check the tree as she disappears into the crowd.

There are people everywhere: families moving too slowly, stopping at every stall for candyfloss, flashing bracelets, bags of bright yellow sweets. There's the smell of burnt sugar, sweat, fat, the tang of hot metal, like overheated brakes. A group of older girls almost walks into me, then veers off, laughing, towards the big wheel. Cigarette smoke blows in and out. Music blares at each ride – disco, jazz, and the fair boys whistle and call out that there are two minutes before their rides start, one minute, then gates clank, more music starts up and someone screams.

Gina threads her way through everything, looking from side to side, past the stalls, past the rides, out to where the generators and cables thump.

I finally catch up with her. 'Let's go on the waltzer,' I say.

She looks at me as if she's forgotten I'm there. 'The waltzer?'

'We always go on that first,' I say. I don't ask why she's gone all the way out to the back of the fair, what she's looking for. Instead I turn and make my way over to the ride, pushing through the crowds, hoping Gina is following behind. Just as I get in the queue I realise I don't have my purse with me. I'm almost at the front and I search my pockets but all I have is a crumpled tissue and a decoration I found that was still hanging on the tree. Just as the woman ahead of me finishes paying, I remember the five-pound note I keep in a tiny, inner pocket in my coat. It's meant to be for emergencies. I've never used it. It's my turn in the queue and the man on the ride asks how many I want. I take out the money and pay for two tickets.

I get on and sit back in the sticky seat. After a few minutes Gina climbs in next to me. Our seat is already tilting at almost a right angle and my stomach starts to feel very light, like it's rising above me. I lean forward and put both hands on the bar. The music starts and the ride jolts. Gina is still sitting back, not even holding the bar, but I can tell she's braced.

We circle around once, the cup spinning slowly on its axis as we go. Gina still isn't holding the bar. Her arms are crossed in front of her. I catch her eye and she gives me a small smile, the kind where only one corner of her mouth rises up. It's her pretend smile – the one she uses for parents or people she passes in the street and doesn't want to speak to – but there's hardly any time to take it in because suddenly the music surges, the lights flare, and we're tipping forwards, spinning backwards and being flung around the ride, our hair whipping across our cheeks. Gina's mouth snaps open but no sound comes out. I shut my eyes. Colours bleed and distort in front of me. The music pulses. Gina slides across the seat and bangs hard into my hip. She grabs at the bar and ends up gripping my wrist, her nails in my skin. We spin three times and I know I'm going to fall out, I'm lifting upwards, my hands are clutching the bar and I open my eyes and see a row of pale, blurred faces. I bang back down. The ride tips then slows. The music cuts out and we come to a shuddering halt. Someone unhooks our bar and we stumble out, the ground rolling under our feet.

'I need to eat something,' I say. I try to walk, but it comes off more like lurching. I follow the smell of onions and burnt coffee. If I don't eat something I'll throw up, I know it. There's a queue. A man at the front doesn't want sugar in his coffee but they've already put sugar in. I have to stop myself pushing him out of the way. Finally it's my turn and I buy a hot dog and a bag of doughnuts. The hot fat seeps through the paper bag, turning it translucent.

I offer the bag to Gina but she shakes her head. I offer again and she takes a doughnut and nibbles at the edges. She wipes her mouth with a napkin after every bite. I eat a doughnut, then half the hot dog, then another doughnut, making sure I don't chew anywhere near my loose tooth. I finish the rest of the hot dog, then lick my fingers one by one to get the last of the mustard and the sugar. Just as I'm about to start on my thumb, someone puts their hand on top of my head. I turn around. It's Mrs Bradley. Her hand is strong and stiff, like a tree root.

'Are my girls having fun?' she asks. There's a wisp of candy-floss trailing from her sleeve. 'Have you been on any rides?'

I finish licking. 'Just the waltzer,' I say.

'With your parents?'

Gina stops eating her doughnut. 'Why would we do that?'

Mrs Bradley smiles quickly. At school we always sat at the front, right by her desk. She gave us gold stars to stick on our books when we got the answers right. 'I saw the merry-go-round earlier,' she says, 'and it reminded me of my girls. Remember when all you wanted to do was be horses? You'd gallop into class and when I asked you a question you'd neigh the answer.'

I nod, but Gina shakes her head. 'I don't remember that,' she says. She looks around and then freezes. The top of her cheeks go even pinker, just for a moment, then fade back to how they were. 'I have to go,' she says. She thrusts the half-eaten dough-nut at me. I catch a glimpse of her jumper as she vanishes back into the crowd.

I turn to follow then stop, but Mrs Bradley waves me on. 'You go,' she says. 'Have fun, OK?'

'I'll look at the merry-go-round later,' I call back, but I don't know if she hears or not.

I walk fast. The fair is even busier now. Queues spill into the walkways and I keep having to stop and go round them. I see a kid from school and then another, bigger group of people I half-recognise. They're sitting on the steps by the big dipper. I almost walk past them but then I see Gina sitting at the top, next to a boy who has his arm slung over her shoulder. I stop. Someone's shoe bangs into my heel. I don't cry out. I don't move. I'm about to back away when Gina sees me and beckons me over. I go slowly, not looking at anyone, and stand near her, at the edge of the steps. I stand very still, like a hare that's caught the scent of something. They're passing a can around and when it comes to me I shake my head, then can't stop watching while Gina drinks. The boy next to her takes the can and finishes it. He has a very thin nose and bloodshot eyes. His hair is so dark it has a blue sheen to it.

I keep licking my lips to make sure there's no sugar left on them, but they taste salty, not sweet, and they sting in the cold.

Gina looks over at me and smiles, properly this time.

I don't smile back.

The group watches everything and everyone that goes past. They watch and then someone says something, or does an imitation, and laughter ripples out, as if a stone has just hit water. No one talks to me and it gets colder and later, until one of the boys turns round suddenly and asks if Gina and I want a ride on anything, we can have a go on anything for free.

Everyone sniggers and the colour comes again into Gina's cheeks, darker this time, more like when she was ten and she grabbed a teacher's hand instead of mine and pulled him around the playground.

I lean in and say something, just to her. She doesn't hear. I say it again. 'Let's go on the dodgems.' I wait for her to get up and come with me, but then everyone is standing up and moving and the boy with his arm around Gina says, 'Good idea. Let's go on the dodgems.'

'Evie,' Gina says. She jerks her head for me to follow. There's nothing else to do except follow. Gina gets in a car next to the boy and someone presses a ticket into my hand and puts me in a car by myself. The music rolls. My car powers up. The man running the ride shoves me off the side. Sparks crackle on the ceiling and I drive.

I circle the edge slowly, looking for Gina. We used to pick someone and follow them mercilessly, ours hands overlapping on the wheel. This time I can pick for myself. I see Gina's car and start following. The boy isn't driving properly. What you're meant to do is go round in a circuit, but he's zigzagging across the floor, ramming into everyone, throwing Gina back in her seat, then reversing and going the other way. His friends are all doing the same. One of them smacks into me from behind and I jolt forward, then spin into the wall. I try to reverse but another car rams me back and my steering locks. I reach out and push off the wall and the wheel turns. I slam my foot on the pedal and aim for Gina's car. I'm almost on them when another car comes in and knocks me sideways and I spin again. I curse and turn the wheel hard. By now I'm leaning my whole weight against the pedal, circling the floor, sparks chipping off above me. I see Gina ahead and I lean forward. She hasn't seen me and I bear down on them, gritting my teeth. Her head is resting on the boy's shoulder. I turn my car so that I can hit them from the side. I'm almost there. I'm already imagining her face, the way she'll look at me when I send them slamming into the wall. I'm five metres away, four metres, and I pump my foot down on the pedal but it feels different, lighter, there's no traction. I pump again but my car is slowing, the music's stopped, the sparks are dying away and I'm stranded in the middle of the floor.

I sit there, my hands still on the wheel, until I'm told I have to get out unless I want to pay for another go. I get up and make my way off the ride. There's a white line across my hands and my knee almost locks from where I've been leaning so hard on the pedal. I go down the steps and stand on the concrete. Behind me, the dodgems start up all over again.

I walk back through the fair. By now it's completely dark and more lights have come on. I step over a crumpled balloon, candyfloss sticks and spilled drinks, which spread across the ground like the fair's tideline.

I can see the vans ahead and I speed up. All I want to do is leave. I try to remember which one we put the tree under. I think it's the middle one and I head straight over. There are two people ahead of me and I realise that it's Gina and the boy. They're walking towards the vans. Gina tilts her face up to look at the boy and for a moment I don't even recognise her. The ground tips and rolls under me. I watch as they disappear round the back of the vans.

A dog barks somewhere behind me – it sounds strange and far away.

Then Mrs Bradley walks past. She's walking towards the exit but the way she's going will take her right between the vans. I take a step forward, stop, then take another. Mrs Bradley keeps going, swinging her arms, stepping over all the sticks and bags. The candyfloss is still stuck to her sleeve. My skin burns under the hot lights. She's going to see Gina, any moment now she will see Gina, and somehow I know that, if Mrs Bradley sees Gina, she'll never call us 'my girls' again, and she'll never touch the tops of our heads or tell us that we used to pretend we were horses.

She's almost there. She's at the first van and her head is about to turn, and suddenly I'm rushing forward, my hand is at my mouth, my tooth is out and there's blood and I must have yelled because now everyone is turning and looking at me instead.

Mrs Bradley comes straight over, and then Gina is there adjusting her jumper. Someone hands me a glass of warm, salty water. Blood swirls back into the glass.

The pain comes suddenly, sharply, and I move my tongue around the gum, feeling the rough, fleshy socket. Someone passes me my tooth – I think it's the boy – and I put it in my pocket because I don't know what else to do with it. It's big and black with dried blood.

Gina puts her mouth to my ear – all beer and doughnuts and bubblegum shampoo – and says, 'Let's go get the tree.'

We slip away from the crowd, away from Mrs Bradley, who is explaining to the boy about the best way to remove teeth. We slide the tree out from under the van and go.

The wind has picked up. It's blowing the sea into white water that gleams in the dark. The fair music throbs behind us, and my mouth throbs in the cold, so I keep it shut.

We take the turning to the coast path, past the fence that marks the edge of the cliff. The path is narrower now, because some of the cliff has fallen away. It's too dark to really see anything but we keep going, following the fence and feeling for when the path turns from gravel to the sand at the start of the dunes. We know the path so well that we automatically step over the cracks and stones and then our feet hit packed sand and we're there.

The dunes have spread since last year. They're lower and flatter, and seem to go on further than I can see. We start walking down, our feet sinking with each step. The sand is very cold and the beach is very quiet. The marram grass rustles, like a group of people waiting for something.

Gina stumbles and puts out her hand. 'Shit, that's sharp,' she says. 'I think I've found the trees.'

We stop and look. I can just make them out – rows of small dark shapes standing stiffly against the wind.

We follow the line until we find a gap. The trees are bare, skeletal, no more than husks. Gina stops and lays our tree down. 'Shall we put it in here?' she says.

I watch the dark blowing sand. It blows over my face and my hair. Suddenly it doesn't seem to matter so much where we put it, or if we put it in at all. The sand will move and bury the trees, the dunes will spread and heap up and flatten again. The trees seem too small; there will never be enough of them.

'I guess so,' I say.

Gina crouches down and starts digging with her hands, scooping out handfuls of sand and piling it up next to her.

I can feel the dunes moving under my feet – big, shifting movements, like an iceberg creaking.

Gina digs hard. She kneels in the sand and leans right into the hole she's making. She works at it steadily, scooping and piling the sand. After a while I kneel down next to her and dig too. The damp grains clog under my nails. We find a rhythm – Gina scoops, then I scoop, one hand after the other. There's just the sound of the sea, and the grass, and our hands in the sand.

The hole is already deep enough but we keep digging anyway, just more slowly. Neither of us stops. But after a while I say, 'That's deep enough now,' and then there's nothing else to do except stop. We stand up and put the tree in the hole and I hold it upright while Gina pushes the sand back around it and stamps it down to keep it in place.

We stand there, not moving, watching the tree.

'Does it hurt?' Gina asks.

Usually I would say something about primary versus secondary lesions – I know all about them from the care home. I would talk about how Mr Samuels, who has been in the home since before I was born, has a gold earring so that, if he'd ever drowned at sea and washed up in another country, he would have had enough money to pay for his own burial. But I don't feel like saying any of that.

'Yes,' I say. 'It hurts.'

The sand blows around us. It's cold and dark. The lights of a fishing boat move past in the distance. I am the first to turn to go. I brush the sand off my hands and start making my way across the dunes. Gina follows me, then, just as we're almost back on the path, she darts away and runs up the side of the highest dune. She runs slowly, fighting against the toppling sand, the way it falls back under her feet. Then she's at the top. I wait on the path. The lights of our bungalows glint in the distance. They look as small and far away as the boat. I think of the sandy streets and the shiny clumps of sea beet. The shortcut down the alley. The cracks in the wall of Gina's front room. I think about those lungs – how they rose up, so full of air, that it was impossible to imagine they didn't really work any more.

Above me, Gina spreads her arms out wide. I look once more at the lights, then I run up the sand and stand next to her. The rows of trees are somewhere behind us. I spread my arms out just as Gina starts running down, and I run too, flying so fast that sand rises up everywhere and we are lost in it; it whirls and kicks up and it's in my eyes, my mouth, it's so loose under my feet that it seems as if there's nothing there.

Gina is ahead of me. She's running so fast that I lose sight of her – one moment she's there, the next she disappears in a scatter of sand. I see an arm, a leg, her pale hair streaming as she moves away, and I am right behind, I am almost right behind, as the dunes below us creak and shift and catch in the wind, like they always do, like they'll always keep doing.

Flotsam, Jetsam,
Lagan, Derelict

MARY AND VINCENT LAYTON lived in a small house that over-looked an empty beach. The beach was wide and rocky – there were rocks the size of doors that had been thrown up by the tide, and smaller stones that banked up in drifts. Rows of low, dark rocks radiated out across the beach like the hands of a clock. These were the worn-down layers where the cliff used to be, before it had been whittled down to its bones.

Their house was painted white, with a porch at the side and a garage at the back. There was a road behind it. In front there was the cliff – still being worn down, still being whittled – but they'd been assured it would not affect them in their lifetime.

They'd moved in over the summer. Finally everything was sorted and in order: their work had reached its natural end point; finances were tied up; their children were married and settled. There were no loose ends. They'd been together for a very long time – they could hardly believe how long really – but now, finally, there were no loose ends.

Vincent had found a job to fill his weekday mornings, doing gardening work for people around the town. Sometimes Mary would go and help but more often she would walk along the cliffs or the beach, or just sit looking out. It was quiet and everything else seemed very far away. There was no TV, no mobile signal. They didn't have to think about anything at all.

One morning Mary was out walking when she saw something glinting further down the beach. She made her way towards it. Clouds hung low in the sky – they were pale, almost yellow, like eyes that were old or tired. The rocks were slippery and she walked carefully – if she fell and broke something then that could be it, and all the work, all the years of planning, would be for nothing. She avoided the places with wet mossy weed, and stepped instead on the fat brown ribbons, which creaked softly under her shoes. It was still early. She'd always woken early but now, instead of lying awake in bed, she got up and came down to the beach.

She crossed the rocks and stepped down onto the sand, which was coarse and flecked with colours. Sometimes it looked bronze. Sometimes it looked silver. It always felt cold, even in the sun, and she often wondered how deep it was.

The glinting thing was half-buried. It was a plastic bottle; one of those small water bottles with ridges all around it. The plastic was tinged blue and the top was sticking up amongst all the stones and shells. It didn't look right. It didn't look like it was supposed to be there. She crouched down, scraped up a handful of sand and pressed it over the top of the bottle. Then she dug up another handful and did the same, until it was completely covered. She stood back and looked. There. She couldn't even tell where it was any more. And later, the tide would take it away for good.

The next morning there were five bottles strewn across the rocks below the house.

Mary stood on the path looking down at them. It was mizzling. The beach seemed flatter and washed of colour, except for the blue of the bottles. She went down the path and over the rocks. They were rectangular five-litre bottles and the plastic was thick and shiny. She collected them one at a time and put them in a pile, then turned and looked back at the cliffs, across the sand, and out at the sea. There was nowhere for the bottles to go. They were too big to bury, and there were too many of them. The tide wouldn't reach that far for hours. She thought about putting them behind one of the big rocks, but she would probably still be able to see them from the house. And, even if she couldn't see them, she would know they were there.

She picked the bottles up awkwardly, holding one under each arm and the rest against her chest, and carried them over the rocks. There was a car park at the other end of the beach which had a bin in it. She crossed the beach and went over to the bin. It was overflowing and there were extra bags stuffed with rubbish on the ground underneath it. She put the bottles down by the bags and turned to leave. The wind knocked one of the bottles over and it fell with a hollow thud. Another one blew back towards the sand. Mary watched it moving. It made a scraping sound as it skidded against the gravel. She picked the bottles up again and carried them back across the beach. She walked up the path towards the house and unlocked the garage. There was a shelf against the back wall and she put them on there, lining them up neatly in a row.

She locked the garage and went inside. Vincent was in the kitchen, making lunch. She went up behind him and put her arms around his waist. He smelled of bonfires and paint. His waist had thickened over the years. So had hers. Sometimes their bones clicked. She leaned into his warm back. He reached his arm around and rubbed her hip.

'Our daughter phoned,' he said. He took four slices of bread out of the bag and put them on plates. The kitchen was small and white and clean. There were white plates in the cupboard, a few white mugs, two bowls and two glasses. They had got rid of almost everything.

'I didn't think we'd given her this number yet,' Mary said.

Vincent put cheese in the bread and cut each sandwich in half. He wiped the crumbs up carefully. 'Something's happening with Jack again.'

Mary watched as Vincent got up the last crumbs with the tip of his finger. He passed Mary her plate and picked up his own.

'Let's eat these in bed,' Mary said. They could do things like that now. They could close all the curtains and afterwards they could sleep until dinner if they wanted to. There was nothing to stop them.

The next morning she took her usual route out of the house and along the path down to the rocks. Before she opened the

112

gate she stopped and scanned the beach. For a moment she thought she saw something glinting and her heart began to beat faster than usual. But it was nothing. The beach was clear and empty. She undid her hair and let it stream out. She started humming. There were shallow pools among the rocks and they rippled in the wind.

She took the long way round, past her favourite rock, which was covered in a dark sheet of mussels.

Her boots crunched on the stones. She passed heaps of seaweed that must have been pushed in by the tide. Some of it was orange, and some was blue, and there were hundreds, maybe thousands, of tiny blue and white shells.

She reached down and picked up some of the seaweed. She liked the way it popped under her hands. But it wasn't seaweed. This was stiff and tough and fraying at the edges. She dropped it and looked at the other piles. They weren't seaweed, none of them were – they were heaps of twisted nylon rope. She crouched down and picked up one of the shells. The edge of it dug into her finger. It was a fragment of plastic. All along the tideline, as far as she could see, the beach was covered in small, sharp fragments.

She turned quickly and went back to the house. The wind knotted her hair into clumps and she tied it up tightly away from her face. She looked through the cupboards for the bin bags. There weren't any left. She went into the garage and found the bucket, which they used to clean the car and the windows. She took the bucket down to the beach with her, knelt in the damp sand, and started picking everything up – rope, plastic, translucent strips of polythene. After a while she stopped doing it piece by piece and scraped up entire handfuls. When the bucket was full she stood up and stretched her legs. Her back was stiff and there was a faint, dull ache in the joints of her hands. She carried the bucket back to the house, opened the garage and emptied it onto the floor. Everything spread in a tangled heap. She locked the garage and went inside.

Vincent was pouring drinks. 'Where've you been?' he asked. He kissed the soft skin on the side of her neck.

'Just my usual walk,' Mary said. She took off her coat.

'You missed lunch,' he told her. He emptied crisps into a bowl and passed them to her.

Mary looked at the clock. Her stomach was empty. When she reached into the bowl the salt stung her fingers.

There was a letter on the table. The envelope was thick and cream-coloured and headed with Vincent's old company's logo. It was still sealed.

Vincent saw her looking and went over to the table, but neither of them opened the letter.

'Why are they writing to you?' Mary said.

'I don't know.'

'I didn't think they needed to write to you any more.'

Vincent took the letter and put it in the drawer underneath the phone. The white kitchen and the white lights made his skin look almost grey. It was Mary who'd first persuaded him to take that job, even though he hadn't wanted to. There were other things he'd wanted to do. She held his hand. Their fingers laced between each other's. Vincent reached over and picked something out of her hair – it was tangled in and it took him a moment to loosen it. It was a strip of blue plastic. That night, when she was getting undressed, she found another strip caught in the cuff of her shirt.

The next day she got up early, took the bucket and went straight to work on the beach. She picked and sifted until her knees throbbed and her hands felt like they were about to seize up. The more she picked up, the more she saw – there were ring pulls, tin lids, bottle caps, tags, rusty springs coiled under stones, watch batteries, translucent beads that she could only see if she squinted, hidden among the grains like clutches of eggs. There were bits of Styrofoam that were exactly the same colour as the sand, and bright specks of glass.

The sun slipped down lower. The tide came in. Finally she stopped and stood up. She'd only covered a few square metres.

When she went to bed there were bits stuck to her feet. When she brushed them off they scattered across the floor and fell down between the boards. She got up and tried to pick them out without waking Vincent. He murmured and reached for her. She got back into bed. Bits of plastic blew in on a draught under the door.

On the day before the rubbish collection Mary took their bin bag from the kitchen and put it by the side of the road. She'd bought a new roll of black bags, and she took them down to the garage, unlocked it, and went in. The room was full. A fetid smell rose up, like something in a ditch that hadn't drained away. The floor was a teeming mass of boxes and crates, ropes, plastic bottles, wet shoes, chipped and broken toys. There were reams of greasy netting with tins and plastic beads and pen

115

lids caught in them; and a heap of oil cans and rubber gloves and mouldy bits of fabric. In the far corner there was a pile of sand and a sieve. Sometimes things looked like sand, but they weren't sand, really.

She stood in the middle of the garage and looked around. There was so much of it – it was piled halfway up the walls. She gripped the roll of bags. What she needed to do was fill each one and then leave them out for the collection. Then, by tomorrow, it would all be gone. She went over to the edge of the pile and started filling the first bag. She filled it quickly, tied the top and started on another, breaking up the boxes and crates, not stopping until everything in the garage was cleared. It took a long time. When she'd finished she dragged the bags outside one by one and put them by the road. A car drove past and slowed down, looking at the vast, toppling pile. Her cheeks burned. But they would be gone by the morning.

Vincent was waiting in the hall. 'We'd better go,' he said. He was buttoning his coat.

'Go?'

'To the Gleesons'. They invited us, remember?'

'I don't remember,' Mary said.

'They said we should go over.'

'Why?'

'I suppose to have a drink. Talk.'

'Talk,' Mary said. 'About what?'

Vincent leaned down and tied his shoes. 'I guess they want to get to know us. Where we lived before, what we're like, what we did.'

Mary leaned back against the wall. 'Before?' she said. She could still smell the rank saltiness on her hands. It was probably on her clothes. She took off her coat and her shoes. She slipped her hand up the back of Vincent's shirt. 'Let's stay in,' she said. His skin was creased and soft. She knew each bone of his spine.

Vincent phoned in for them and they spent the evening listening to music and eating leftovers from the fridge, with the radiators turned up high.

The wind picked up and surged all night. The tiles clattered like bits of stone falling off the cliff. Hail chipped at the windows. Mary lay awake listening to the waves hitting against the beach. She thought about the bags out on the road. The palm tree scratched against the wall. She sat up suddenly. Where would it all go, after it had been collected? It wouldn't really be gone, would it? It would just be somewhere else. It would be somewhere else, instead of here. Maybe, eventually, some of it would end up back on the beach. Her heart beat hard, almost painfully. She couldn't think about that. She'd done what she could. Eventually she lay back down and closed her eyes.

She slipped out early the next morning, while Vincent was still asleep. There were two messages from their daughter on the answerphone. The red light flashed slowly.

When she opened the front door it hit against something. She pushed harder but it still wouldn't open more than a few inches. There was something on the other side – she could almost see it through the letter box. She shoved harder and the door finally opened. There was a pile of wet netting slumped against it. She pushed it away with her foot and went out. The grass was strewn with rope and shoes and tins. Some of the bin bags had ripped open, some had tipped over and come untied, some had rolled down the path and burst. Plastic had been flung across the road. There were bottles and strips of cardboard caught in the hedge; packets flapped on the ground like injured birds. There was a rubber glove pressing against the downstairs window.

Mary stood in the middle of the garden for a long time. Then she turned, picked up her bucket, and walked slowly down to the beach.

The sand was churned; stones had been flung around into new trenches and drifts. Water trickled off the cliff in thin streams, as if a cloth were being wrung out. Mary looked across the rocks, deciding which way to go first. There was something bright further ahead, on the other side of the beach – a row of something that she couldn't quite make out. The rocks on that side were taller, more jagged. She didn't normally go that way. The early-morning sun flashed on whatever it was. They looked like discs. Mary closed her eyes but still saw the shapes on the backs of her eyelids.

There were no flat places to rest her feet so she just kept going – stepping quickly from rock to rock without giving herself time to lose balance. Finally she could see what they were – it was a mass of hub-caps, piles of them, like a stranding. Some had been thrown up on top of the rocks. Others were cracked in half. Her heart beat hard again. There were so many of them. More were washing in and rolling at the edge of the tide.

She left the bucket and picked up as many as she could, tucking them under her arms and holding a stack in both hands. Then she turned and made her way across the rocks. She would leave them by the path, then go back for more.

She was almost on the sand when she slipped. She reached out with her foot but found nothing. The hub-caps clattered down. She stretched out her arm but still there was nothing, then her wrist twisted against the ground and something rough grated against her cheek. The stones and the sand were very cold.

When Vincent found her she'd managed to drag herself so that she was almost on the path. He leaned her against him, taking her weight, and walked her slowly back to the house, lifting her with each step.

'What have you been doing?' he asked. He gently prised the hub-cap out of her hands.

She couldn't get out of bed. Vincent brought her breakfast on a tray in the morning, then, when he got back from work, he made lunch and they ate together, sitting propped up on the pillows. He brought in the radio and rubbed her swollen ankle while they listened.

The room was small and bare and white. Once, a piece of plastic, or maybe a wrapper, caught on the window and flapped in the wind. Mary closed her eyes. When she opened them again it had gone. The walls smelled like fresh paint and she lay there, breathing it in. This was how it was meant to be: the

119

quiet, the sea somewhere outside the window. She slept deeply and for a long time.

One lunchtime she woke up from a nap and Vincent wasn't there. 'Vincent?' she called. 'Are you back?' She was hungry. She tried getting out of bed but as soon as she put any weight on her foot it wrenched and gave way. She sat back down. It grew slowly dark. Finally she heard the front door open and a few moments later Vincent came in. His hands were cold but the tops of his cheeks looked very hot.

'It's late,' Mary said.

'It was work,' he told her. 'I overran doing the Millers' garden.' He brought her tea and a sandwich and straightened the covers. He sat next to her and switched on the radio. He turned the volume up high.

After a while he said, 'Do you ever think about it?'

'What?' Mary asked.

'It was your parents' and I …'

Mary must have moved suddenly because a shot of pain went through her foot. 'Why are you talking about that?' she said.

'I just thought about it today.'

'We said we wouldn't,' she told him.

Vincent nodded. He turned and patted her pillow so that it was more comfortable. 'I should have checked it all out,' he said. 'I don't know why I didn't check.'

'We said we wouldn't go over it any more,' Mary said. All that was done with now. She hadn't thought about it for a long time.

Vincent was late back again the next day, and the day after that. He fell asleep straight after dinner but woke up through the night, his legs and arms moving restlessly.

The following morning he was gone before she was awake. Mary's breakfast was on the bedside table. She drank cold tea and ate cold toast. The phone rang. She got up and put her foot carefully on the floor. There was a dull ache but she could stand. She walked slowly through the house. The phone stopped ringing. The message light was flashing red. The kitchen was clean and quiet. There was another unopened letter from Vincent's company on the table.

She went out and turned towards the living room. The door was closed. It was never closed. The phone rang again and she went back into the kitchen. She watched it ringing for a moment, then picked it up. 'Hello?' she said. She nodded slowly, said a few words, then put the phone down. Vincent hadn't been showing up for work.

She opened the living-room door. The room was full. Every shelf, every inch of floor space, every chair, was covered with things from the beach. The hub-caps were stacked in tall piles, like coins. There were fruit crates, balls of rope, a bag overflowing with what looked like computer parts. There were fishing buoys – some orange, some green, some bleached to no colour at all. Sheets of plastic leaned against the window, casting a warped light. The room smelled stale, but also humid. Water droplets collected and rolled down the walls.

She went over to the window and looked out. Vincent was standing near the edge of the water, on the far side of the beach, staring at something. She closed the living-room door, put on her shoes, tied them carefully over her ankle, and went outside. The wind was picking up again. The tiles clacked. The palm tree was frayed. There were bin bags stuffed full in the porch and more along the side of the path.

She went down to Vincent and slipped her arms around his waist. He put his hand on her hip.

'It was just there,' he said. 'I came down and it was just there.'

Mary followed where he was looking, past the rocks, and over towards the water. At first she thought it was another rock. It towered up next to the cliff. Then she saw dark red metal. There was some kind of writing painted on the side. It was a shipping container, almost the size of the house, draped in seaweed and barnacles. It was padlocked. The metal was thick and corrugated. One side was bent inwards, like a chest when someone is holding their breath.

'I thought it was going to be different,' Mary said. She held Vincent tighter and leaned into his back.

'Maybe by the morning …' Vincent said.

But they both knew it would still be there in the morning. It was, perhaps, unmovable.

They stood there, together, watching it.

The Life of a Wave

All waves begin as nothing more than a wrinkle, called a cat's paw – a crease in the surface of the water caused by a gust of wind.

You're lying on a blanket on the hot sand and shadows move across your eyes. Above you, there is the sky and in it there's a hard, white crescent. You reach out and try to cram it in your mouth. Sand scratches your elbows. The blanket smells sweet and dusty and there are small stones under it. Something is drumming somewhere. It's deep and regular and it sounds close one moment and far away the next. You can't see it. You rock and kick your feet but you still can't see it. You roll onto your side. The drumming comes through the ground and into your ear.

A shadow moves and grows bigger and your father sits down next to you. Heat radiates off him in waves. There's a lot of bright orangey hair on his legs and neck and when you pull on it he sucks in his breath and says, 'He's trying to kill me.' His hand is hot and damp when it unclenches your fist. You try and grab again. You want him to come closer but he's holding something and now he's looking at that instead. It's another body. It's red and blue and he's pulling it over himself. The sun beats down. He sweats and breathes heavily. Sometimes he grunts. He pulls the rubbery legs up over his knees and his elbows fly out. Your mother says, 'Merl, mind the baby.' She puts down her book. Your father swoops towards you, except it's not your father – it's some kind of dark bird. There's no skin, there's no hair. It slips and creaks under your fingers. It smells hot and burning and you cry out because he's disappeared.

In the night he stumbles into your room to quieten you. His face looms, then turns away, like the moon's does. Sometimes he paces the house and your eyes follow him as he crosses from room to room.

He shows you the sea from your window. He lifts you up ('By God,' he says, 'your heart's going about a thousand times a second') and there is a glimpse of it in the distance. It glints and it's different to the sky and that is where he always goes. He holds you for a long time, until he lets out a shout because you've peed down his wrist.

The deep galumphing noises are the same as the ones in his chest.

Your mother goes away for the day and your father looks after you by himself. When you cry he gives you a chamois leather to hold, and you clutch it, gumming the soft corners. You fall asleep. When you wake up you're on the beach. You reach out and grab for him. There's a dent in the sand where his surfboard has been, and footprints disappearing down towards the sea.

This is the story that's told: an hour passed and then another. You slept and then woke up and the friend of your father's who was watching over you, knowing nothing about babies, bought you an ice cream which melted over your legs. You were taken to the lifeguard hut and someone put a jacket over you. You clutched the chamois leather. Eventually your father came back in, wet and dripping, elated: the waves were glassy, he caught a tube at the end. When the lifeguard handed you over your father blinked, laughed, then slapped everyone on the back. He'd completely forgotten you existed.

The wave grows as it comes into conflict with the surface tension of the water. This is called the capillary wave.

You grow up with a language you think everyone knows: lumpy, crumbly, clean, hollow, walling up. You know reef breaks and shore breaks. You know of faraway, gigantic waves: Waimea, Mavericks, Pipeline. To you they are as strange and magical as Lapland. You know that to drop in on someone, to steal their wave, is the worst crime. In town, when your mother says that

125

the two of you could drop in on her friend, you scream and won't go in the door.

When you stand at the edge of the water the waves tug and hiss at your feet. They break suddenly; rearing up then smashing down, like the jars you throw as hard as you can at the recycling centre. Your father wades in ahead of you and, after a moment, you follow. Seaweed wraps around your toes. Something sharp hits your ankle. You're in over your waist. Cold water flushes down your trunks. You turn and look back. There's your mother on the sand, holding your baby sister. They look small and far away. You take another step forwards, then turn back again. Everything onshore looks different. You hardly recognise it. You wave, and someone waves back, distantly.

You find an injured crab and bring it home in your pocket. You put it under your bed and bring it crisps and grapes. After a few days you forget to check. When you look again, the crab has died. The smell stays in the room for weeks.

You lose your chamois leather. You look everywhere for it, then crawl and hide under the table. Your mother asks what's wrong. A few minutes later your father comes in from the garden. His voice is louder than usual. His eyes don't quite meet yours. He leans down to you – his face is huge, it crowds out everything; it's flecked with golden stubble and bits of soap and shaving nicks – and then he presents the chamois with a flourish. You take it slowly. It's damp and it smells strong and different and there's wax around the edges.

Your mother reads you a book about the moon. You can't stop thinking about it. You get up at night and look at it out of your window – sometimes you can see the face clearly, sometimes it's sly and shadowy and you can't make it out at all.

When he waxes his surfboard you stand behind and watch. He leans down and scrapes the old wax off. The flakes curl onto the ground like bits of grey snow. Then he wipes the board down with a rag and a bottle of something called turpentine. When he's finished you're allowed to rub on the new layer. The block of wax is shaped like a lady's you-know-what.

When he puts on his wetsuit it's your job to pass him his zip. The zip is very long and he can't reach it by himself. You do it carefully and solemnly. It is your task alone.

Finally, you're given a lesson. It's so windy that you can hardly carry your end of the board across the beach. The waves don't look that big from the car park but as soon as you step into the water they seem to tower over you. Spray stings your face. The board knocks against your shoulder. You can't even climb onto it. You finally get one leg on it and then you slip off the side. A wave flips the board and knocks it against your neck. 'Move forward,' your father shouts. You can hardly hear him over the wind. 'Move forward.' His main teaching technique is to say the same thing, just louder. 'Where?' you ask. Another wave hits you and you roll under, swallowing what feels like lungfuls. Your throat and stomach burn. You come up retching and try to climb on again. The board seems huge and awkward now that you're on it. The waves are relentless. Your father is talking to someone who's just about to paddle out. They shout and laugh. They talk about yesterday's waves. He nods to someone else. He knows everyone. The waves don't knock him off balance; they seem to pass through him, glistening. You fall off again. The board thwacks you across the arse and you rip off your leash, trip, half-running, half-wading back into shore. Your father picks up the board and starts to follow you. Behind him, a perfect set develops. He turns to watch it. You know what he wants – he wants to go back out and catch them. He looks at you. You fold your arms and demand to be taken home.

In the summer he hoses off the salt and leaves his wetsuit dripping on the line all night. By the morning it's dry and stiff and ready to put on again.

Water particles in a wave don't move forward: the wave moves through the water particles, which stay in exactly the same place – these are called rolling particles.

In the winter, you watch him break ice off his wetsuit before he puts it on. You're in the steamy kitchen, eating breakfast and playing slaps with your sister. He chips away the ice from his hat, his gloves, his boots. His leash is an icicle. You shake your head and turn away.

You catch him phoning in sick to work. You should have left for school already but you've forgotten your PE kit and have to go back. He isn't sick but he's been working ten-hour shifts at the warehouse, coming in late smelling of sweat and dust. He puts the phone down and unbuttons the top of his shirt. He sees you standing there and something passes across his eyes – not fear exactly, not exactly distaste. You see yourself suddenly as an interloper: skinny, buck-toothed, always hungry, a rash of coppery freckles on your forehead. 'I forgot my bag,' you tell him, holding it up for evidence. He nods, watching you carefully, then his bear paw comes down and ruffles your hair, boom, boom, kneading his fingers into the back of your neck.

You decide you will be an astronaut. The moon seems very still. Nothing up there would drum and knock you off your feet; you would just float, silently.

You find a mouse behind the fridge. The cat must have brought it in and then lost it. The mouse has made a dusty nest and had five babies. You put them all in a shoebox and keep them in your room. The first few days you dig up worms but the mice don't seem interested. You switch to cheese but they don't eat that either. After a while you forget about them, and when you remember and open the box, they're all dead.

In school you learn that to be an astronaut you must not only be top of the class, but also fit, strong and mentally resilient. You start doing sit-ups every morning. You sit in your tiny wardrobe, very hunched and still, for half an hour every day.

One Saturday morning your father takes your sister down to the beach for her first lesson. She has your old wetsuit and your old polystyrene board. You wait in the house. You can't settle to anything. You walk down to the library, where your mother works. She's laughing with the other librarian about some graffiti a kid has left in a *Where's Wally?* book. She shows you but you don't crack a smile. You grab the first book you see and walk home. You pace the house. When you hear the car you run upstairs and lie on the bed with the book. The doors thump shut. There's no other sound – no talking, no laughing. You turn the pages without reading them. Then your sister laughs and your father squirts water at her with the hose. You close the book slowly.

You can do twenty sit-ups, and you can sit in the wardrobe for an hour – any longer than that and your hips cramp up.

He misses the school play. You've been cast as a servant and your sister is Juliet. Your sister is secretly in love with Romeo – a boy called Jackson who wears henna tattoos. The seat next to your mother is empty. She puts her coat and bag on it. Halfway through, there's a noise at the back of the auditorium and your father comes in with dripping hair. 'Did I miss much?' he asks.

He has a black eye. 'Someone dropped in on me,' he whispers loudly. Everyone has to stand up as he moves down the row. His hair drips onto the floor. Your sister flushes, almost forgets her lines. 'Is that your dad?' Romeo mouths.

Your sister stops her surfing lessons. The wetsuit and the polystyrene board are sold.

You can spend two hours in the wardrobe. The time seems to fly by.

His black eye takes two months to disappear. First it's purple, then green, then yellow. Your mother says he deserves it, then gently holds a bag of peas on it for a few minutes every day.

Things always seem to happen when your father is out in the water. For example, your sister falls through the downstairs window. You were chasing her around the house because she used your telescope without asking and now, somehow, it's broken. She wasn't even looking at stars – she was trying to see if she could spy on her friend on the other side of town. There's a lot of glass but not as much blood as you might expect. When the ambulance comes everything goes very quiet. You're too old to do it, but you hide under the kitchen table. The ambulance doors shut and everyone leaves. The house is dark. When your father comes home he opens the door and calls out, then he switches on the lights, hums, cleans off his wetsuit and hangs it on the line. He turns on the radio to a station you don't recognise. He sings along. He opens the fridge, heaps food onto a plate and eats with his hands: tearing bread, wiping sauce with his fingers. You crawl out. He jumps and bellows, almost chokes on a slice of cold chicken. You explain where everyone is. It takes him a while to understand. He hasn't noticed the broken window. The calm glassiness in his eyes slowly fades. He sits down and rubs his jaw, then drives you both to the hospital.

The next time he goes in your rabbit, Millicent, is run over by a motorbike.

Another time a swarm of bees comes down the chimney and gets trapped in the living room. A bee catches in your sleeve and stings you on the wrist, even though you were trying to help it. The sting swells to the size of a planet.

'How?' your father asks each time. 'How has it happened?' You don't know it yet but what he means is: how can life, this other life, have carried on so drastically without him, while he was just drifting on his board, a basking shark slipping under him like a submarine?

Each time he paces the house. No one speaks to him. Everything has been taken care of without him – he has not-helped, he is not-needed. He frowns and mutters to himself. He looks around but no one looks at him. He mutters again. Then, suddenly, he runs out. He takes the box of bees, which your mother stunned with smoke while wearing a snorkel, and leaves

132

it at the bottom of the mean neighbour's garden. He draws rude, elaborate pictures over your sister's cast. He digs a grave for the rabbit under the buddleia, puts on a suit, and conducts a service: prayers, hymns, a soaring eulogy that speaks of her kindness, her penchant for cereal and how she stared at herself, almost smiling, in the glass of the oven.

When you walk past the beach on your way into town, your eyes scan the water. There are many small, dark dots drifting out the back. It's hard to tell which one he is. There he is, no there, no there, no there.

The drag of the water against the seabed begins to slow the wave down.

You bring home a girlfriend. She has waves in her hair and a nose that broke and healed crookedly. Over dinner, your father is loud and animated. The light shines on his orange hair; his skin looks darker, more golden. He stands up to speak and moves his arms in wide, expansive gestures. He presses more food on everyone and makes them all laugh. There's roast chicken and he pulls the skin off in sheets and rolls them delicately – usually you both do it. He looks over at you. You don't do it. You eat quickly and ask to be excused. Just as you're getting up he launches into a long, complicated anecdote about you – the time that you locked yourself out of the house and tried to get in through the roof hatch. The mean neighbour saw you and phoned the police. Your girlfriend laughs in all

133

the right places, but this actually happened to your sister, not to you. No one mentions it. You roll your eyes and say, 'Yeah, good one, Dad.' Then you go upstairs with your girlfriend and into the wardrobe. It's good that you got so much practice in that cramped space. You hear your father calling to you, and you both sit there, silently, the light striping you through the slats, your underwear slung over your old bears and books and space rockets.

You get up late and come home late. By the time you're up, he's already left for work. By the time you get back, he's asleep, sometimes on the sofa, his head tipping up against the cushions, his mouth slightly open as if he's about to speak.

His wetsuit drips on the line. It has a rip down one side and the gloves are fraying.

You are applying for courses in astrophysics. They are competitive and far away. Your girlfriend tells you to stop worrying. She takes off her shirt. She closes your books. When the exams come you race through the papers, writing essays, ticking multiple choices. You don't look up. You reach the final section. It doesn't seem familiar. The questions are strange and unfamiliar. You haven't revised for this – there is a whole section you haven't revised for. You put down your pen. You look up.

Your father is having some trouble at work. He has to go in at weekends, and in the evenings. There's something wrong with the accounts, there's talk of cutting back, redundancies, but he doesn't want to talk about it. What he does want to talk about is the rumour of the fifteen, maybe twenty-foot wave that's going to hit the coast in the next few weeks. He's going to try and ride it. He asks if anyone will be coming to watch. Your mother will be away, visiting friends. Your sister shakes her head. You're about to do the same but then you stop yourself. Exams were a long time ago, the summer is dragging. You have nothing to do except wait. You say that you'll go. Your father glowers – his whole body darkens and seems to fill the room – he glowers like he does when he wants to disguise being pleased.

On the day of the wave you can hear the sea from the front door. He packs the car and puts the board across the front seat. You sit in the back, behind him, like a little kid. Your father talks non-stop, almost babbling, about angles of approach, velocity, the height of the drop. When you get there, the car park is full. There are surfers everywhere and lots of people with cameras. He gets out, unpacks and gets changed. He's still talking. He puts on his boots and gloves. You do up your coat. He locks the car and you follow him down the beach. The waves are huge already – they're dark green and they break like thunder rolling. Your father turns back and looks at the car. Something in his face reminds you of the time he thought there was an intruder in the house and he came out carrying a rolling pin. Or the time he was cornered by that weird dog

135

down the road and it was crawling towards him. 'It's big,' you say. He nods, staring out at the water. 'You don't have to do it,' you tell him. He turns and looks at you, then back at the car. Then someone waves at him and calls him over and the next moment he's gone – he's gone so quickly you don't have time to pass him his zip. You see him laughing, slapping someone on the back. Someone else does up his zip.

There are hands over your eyes and your girlfriend says, 'Guess who?' You say you have no idea: then, when she takes her hands away, you pretend you still don't recognise her. Her smile falters. For some reason you think of those mice in the dark box. You smile and kiss her fingers. You slip your hand into the back pocket of her jeans. You watch the waves. The results came in this morning and you've failed an exam. You haven't told anyone. You're not sure exactly what you'll do, but you guess you'll take up another course instead – there's ones in business or IT that look OK, at the same place your girlfriend is going, which is probably better anyway, it's probably much better this way.

It's impossible to tell how big the wave is until you see your father begin to paddle into it. It rises higher and he rises with it. Then he's up on his board and dropping. For a moment you lose sight of him in the speed and tumult. The roar is almost deafening. Spray hits against your face. The moon is thin as a bone. You see him wipe out for the first time.

While the base of the wave slows, the top rushes on, becoming steeper and more unstable. In a green wave, this top is glassy and smooth, like a mirror.

In your office at your work placement, there's a lot of paperwork to get through. It seems so much, it's like an impossible wave. Sometimes, when you work late, you look out of the window and see the moon and the stars in the yellow-black sky. All the telescopes at observatories around the world will be looking up at this exact moment: Arecibo, Coonabarabran, Jodrell Bank. They are as magical and far away as Lapland. You unpack the food your new girlfriend has made you – cold chicken, tomatoes, bread – it's delicious. You've only been with her for two months. You count down the minutes until you can see her.

One night you're driving in the dark on your way to her parents' house. She's already there. You haven't met her parents yet. You're spending the whole weekend. It's a long drive and you're running late. There's a meteor shower scheduled which is going to start at any moment. You keep driving. You glimpse something bright falling in the rear-view mirror. You don't stop. You're not even halfway yet and the roads are busy. The meteor shower is about to peak. You're very late now. You pull over, stop the car, and get out.

When you visit other people's houses – friends from university, from work, your girlfriend's parents – what you notice is that their fathers are usually there. They are in the kitchen or in the garden or in the garage with drills and paint. They sit and try to talk to you, and you become strange and tongue-tied. 'Uh,' you say. 'Pardon?' They are not rushing around because the tide and the swell and the wind have all come together to make the best possible conditions at an inconvenient time. They are not out chasing anything.

Sometimes, when you're half-asleep, you think you can hear the sea. Sometimes it's the wind in the roof. Sometimes it's your heart beating. Sometimes it's the sound of the motorway in the distance, that restless, relentless thrumming.

Your sister is having a baby. You go and see her and touch her stomach. You can feel the foot sticking out in there. She's grown her hair long and has a dog that lies across her feet. At first you play with the dog a lot, but it always does the same things and soon you get bored and ignore it. The dog seems to understand and shuffles away. There's a scar on your sister's arm from where she fell through the window – it feels like a long time ago, but also not very long ago at all. She craves meat even though she's a vegetarian and you break her in, you roast her a chicken and show her how to peel the skin off in sheets and roll them up. 'You look just like him when you do that,' she tells you.

138

The wave collapses under its own weight. It topples and begins to break.

He has an injury. You phone up and he answers and speaks in a subdued voice. 'Pardon?' he says all the time. 'What?' He's always had terrible surfers' ear, where the bone, after long immersion in cold water, begins to grow to try and stop the water getting in. He was once told his ears were about fifty per cent covered, but now it's more like sixty-five. 'Your injury,' you shout. 'What is it?' It turns out that he hurt his back hanging out the washing in cold weather and he hasn't been in the sea for months. 'Months?' you say. He passes the phone to your mother.

You pull in out the front and go inside. The house is tidy, spotless actually. There's no surf kit on the line. There's no wax or turpentine anywhere. Over the years he's had a few accidents and injuries: the black eye, a cut leg, a broken wrist, concussion, but nothing stopped him going back in before. You pace the house, crossing from room to room. Finally you find him upstairs, in his bedroom, where there's a new TV. He's sitting up watching it. 'Hanging out the washing?' you say. He shows you his new favourite programme. It's about people who buy old crappy cars and then do them up so that they look new. 'They made that one turn out alright,' he keeps saying. 'They made that turn out alright, didn't they?'

The moon is almost full. It's very pale, very yellow. He says that when he hears the waves now they sound like windows smashing. 'OK, Dad,' you tell him. 'OK.'

You catch him bending down to clip the lawn, his back strong and flexible, his arms stretching out. He reaches up to the top shelf in the kitchen and twists when he backs out of the driveway in the car.

Your girlfriend rings you. Her voice is different – higher, she's talking faster, she's trying to tell you something important. Your hands start to shake. You think you know what she's saying. 'It's definite,' she says. 'I did the test twice.' She cries and then starts to laugh. You do the same. You definitely know what she's saying. The room suddenly feels very small. You get up and look out of your old bedroom window. By God, your heart is going about a thousand times a second. Maybe this is what going into space feels like.

The wind direction is good, the tide is right, the swell is small but likely to pick up. You pack the wetsuits and the boards in the car, get your father and drive him down to the sea. You park up and look out. He buries his chin into his chest. The skin around his jaw seems looser, there's more weight across his stomach and face. He's still a big man but the extra weight seems to diminish him somehow, as if he's slowly disappearing. He watches the sea, leaning back in the seat, holding one hand in the other. You tell him your news. He sits there, staring

140

out. 'Was I …' he says. Then he stops. 'I'll have to find a new chamois leather,' he says. There's a shaving nick on his face, golden stubble, bits of soap. You tell him he should go in. He shakes his head. He looks tired. 'There's going to be a few waves coming,' you tell him. He shakes his head again, but you get up and go to the boot and start taking everything out. You get ready. After a while your father gets ready and you both walk down to the water. You stand there. The waves seem so much bigger down here – you'd forgotten that. They seem to tower over you. They boom and snap. Neither of you move; you just stand there, holding your boards. 'Bit small,' your father says. You reach out and pass him his zip. He passes you your zip. When you step into the white water he carries on, paddling out until he's nothing more than a dark dot.

A wave comes in. You climb onto the board and slide off. You try again and it flips over and thwacks you across the arse. The wave knocks into you and pushes you down. The board jolts away and gets dragged in the backwash. Something sharp hits your ankle. Cold water flushes down your wetsuit. You look back at the beach. Everything onshore looks different and far away. You hardly recognise it. Another wave comes in, and then another. You climb onto the board and start to paddle. The white water is coming, it's pounding into you, and then the board is lifting and you're going, you're shooting forwards and you get one knee up, then half-stand, shakily. For a moment you're above the noise and the tumult. Everything is pushing and pulling but you are suspended, still: a force, for a moment, that is unacted upon. Then you fall off, roll, and come up retching. Your throat and stomach burn. You stand up and steady your board. You look for your father. He's still drifting out the back, even though a set has just washed in. The wind is picking up. Another, bigger set develops and breaks but he leaves those as well. With each wave that passes he disappears, appears, disappears, appears. 'Catch one then,' you say. 'Why don't you catch one?' He leaves another one. Someone next to him catches it, but the wave flattens out halfway in and leaves them floundering. Still your father is out there, waiting. He leaves another wave, and another. He's watching them as they form; none of them are right yet, none of them are exactly right. You don't know it yet but he's waiting for the best one, the one that will be perfect. The one that will bring him in right in front of you, finally, in triumph.

Standing Water

SO THERE'S THESE NEIGHBOURS that live out past the quarry, down a rough track that goes nowhere and then stops at the edge of a slushy field. It's low ground out there, and it rains more days than it doesn't, giving the place a bottom-of-the-well kind of feel. The nettles grow to neck height.

There's her house, and then, almost opposite, there's his. They can see each other easily enough – whose car is there, whose lights are on. They can see through each other's windows. There aren't any trees. There aren't any other houses. No one passes by. It's just the two of them, but they haven't spoken since the ditch started overflowing.

The ditch runs along the bottom of the track, and there's a drain in the middle that serves both their houses. The drain is always blocked. When it rains, the water fills the ditch and starts spilling over. It rushes along the track and over the grass and pools outside their front doors. It happens every month, every week. The drain spits and gurgles and the water gushes out, greasy and rabbit-coloured. It smells like a jug that's been holding flowers too long – that slick dark bit that gets left around the edges. Sometimes it seeps under their doors. Sometimes it seeps through their walls. In winter it freezes to a gristly crust. In summer midges spawn and dance over it.

But they never get it fixed. He thinks it's on her land and so she should be the one to do it – he remembers seeing some kind of clause in some kind of document relating to the boundary line, although he's misplaced the paperwork. She says it's closer to his house and so it's his responsibility – she's measured the distance and there's at least four inches in it.

She puts out sandbags. He buys a stiff broom and pushes the water away with sharp jabs. If they're ever out the front at the same time they carry on in silence. She swings her heavy grey plait down behind her back. It's like the pulley on a church bell except nothing chimes. He pulls the hood of his coat down low, so that only the frayed wires of his beard can be seen. Sometimes someone will shake their fist. When their doors slam, they echo across the fields.

The months pass, and then the years. They watch each other, they know each other's small routines – how, on Mondays, she leaves the house at eleven and comes back at two, carrying a plastic bag with bread and some kind of bottle in it. How he stays in every day of the week except Sundays, when he goes out early and comes back at midnight on the dot, with dark lines below his eyes. How she never watches TV. How he leaves

144

his bedroom light on all night. How she crushes tins so hard for the recycling that they split in the middle. How he carefully cleans his spades. How she checks twice that she's locked the door behind her. How he checks that he's locked his door three times.

Once in a while she looks out and sees that all his curtains are shut. They can stay like that for weeks.

Once in a while he smells smoke and sees that she's having a bonfire; tearing out bits of paper from folders and feeding them into the flames. The cinders land on his van. They're as big as fists.

He knows what days she washes her hair.

She knows what day he changes his bed.

Sometimes, at night, he thinks he sees a torch glinting around the track.

Sometimes, at night, she thinks she sees a torch glinting around the field.

If a delivery comes for her when she isn't in, he doesn't take it. He asks for it to be left outside her door instead. Often it gets wet. Sometimes deliveries don't seem to arrive at all.

When he goes out on Sundays, she flattens the gravel outside her house, which his van has churned into divots. She picks up the sharpest bits and puts them on his drive.

The months pass and then the years. Still it rains most days. The drain blocks up and the ditch overflows and water pools in front of their houses.

One evening, at the tail end of winter, the rain is coming down as thick and heavy as a tap on full throttle. The gutters pour. The drops are fat and grimy and smear on the windows. She's inside slicing the skin off potatoes, when she hears something scraping, then a thud. She goes over to the window and glimpses a torch somewhere down the track. The torch goes out. She starts on the potatoes again. The rain drums even louder. She cuts each potato and throws the pieces into a pan of cold water. They sink to the bottom. Something moves in the pelting rain and when she looks up he's there, outside the window, staring in. His eyes are pale and watery. She puts the knife down slowly. She goes to the door and opens it a few inches. He's hunched by the wall, wearing his mac and carrying a spade. There's mud up his legs and his back, and along both sleeves. His hood is streaming. Water runs off the bones of his face.

'Have you got a spade?' he says.

She squints out past the door. The light outside is dark brown, almost green, mud-coloured. She can hardly see him through it. 'Why?' she says.

'It's blocked.'

'It's always blocked.'

He turns and looks down the track. 'It's pouring over.' His voice is strange, lower than she remembers; it catches in his throat as if there's water bubbling in it.

She closes the door an inch and stands behind it.

He pulls his hood down further. 'I can't do it by myself.'

She sees that his spade is clagged with dirt. 'You've been trying to fix it?' she says.

He turns again and looks down towards the ditch. He clutches the spade. The skin on his fingers is damp and crinkled. He opens his mouth and it looks, for a moment, as if a trickle of something dark comes out, but it must just be mud from his hood. He closes his mouth, swallows, and walks back onto the track. His spade scrapes on the ground. Water pours over the tops of his boots. He blurs into the rain and disappears.

She opens the door wider and stands there, looking out. She can't really see anything except the rain. The water looks higher than usual – there's a pool under the door already and it's still rising. She looks back at her kitchen. The pool of water starts spreading. She unhooks her coat from the peg, pulls on her boots and gets her spade from the garage – it's rusty and buckling but it will have to do. She steps into the water and follows him down to the ditch, bending her head against the force of the downpour. He's walking slowly, almost bowed over, with one leg dragging. There are slabs of mud under his boots.

The ditch is overflowing fast. It's gritty and thick and slopping out like bathwater going over the rim. He bends down and starts digging, bringing out spadefuls and throwing them over his shoulder. The ditch looks much wider than it was before. The bank has collapsed down one side, water is flooding out, and there's mud and weeds choking everything. She leans in and digs, scooping out stones and roots. Sludge smears up her legs and hands.

After a while she notices that he keeps stopping and stretching his back. He tries to straighten it but it's stooped, as if there's something heavy pressing down on it. Sometimes he turns and spits behind him. His spit looks muddy. There's mud in his teeth and under his nails. It looks like there's water brimming under his coat.

She digs deeper, scooping out spade after spade of dirt and crushed nettles. The rain is like hands pummelling. It roars in her ears. The pile of mud is growing behind her, but the ditch is so deep and there's so much slipped mud, it doesn't seem like she's even cleared half of it yet.

'When did this happen?' she says.

Another bit of the bank slides into the water – a chunk of clay and roots that calves off stickily.

She keeps digging and the shape of the ditch becomes clearer. It is bigger. The sides have been scraped and cleared and a channel has been dug through the bank. She digs again and finds a section of pipe that wasn't there before. It definitely wasn't there before. She digs around it. The pipe is long. It's been laid in the channel and comes out onto her side of the track. Water is pouring out of it and diverting straight onto her land. She digs again. The pipe isn't finished, but there are more sections in there ready to be joined together, and more channels that, once they're finished, will siphon all the water off in the same direction.

She looks at his muddy coat, the mud on his spade. Suddenly she knows exactly what he's been doing.

'You underhanded bastard,' she says. She clenches the spade, turns around, and raises it in the air.

He's gone. He was standing right next to her and now there's nothing. The rain is dark and cold. She scans the track, the field, but there's no one there. She looks at the bank – there are

148

no footprints where he was standing. The mud is smooth and clear, the grass is untrampled. She curses and swings her spade down deep into the water. It hits something solid. It doesn't feel like rock, it feels softer than that, but harder than the mud.

She wades into the ditch to get a better look. The water sucks at her boots. She digs in again and hits the same thing. It's down underneath where the bank has collapsed. It's big. She prods carefully, loosening, lifting the mud around it. She gets her spade in one more time but can't prise it loose. She kneels down and puts her arms into the water. It's deep. It comes up past her elbows. The chill comes up past her neck. She reaches down and feels around and her fingers catch at something. She grabs it and pulls. It's heavy, and it seems to be caught down there, wedged in under the piles of slipped mud. She pulls harder, leaning back with all her weight. The thing shifts. She reaches down, untangles a root, and moves some hard lumps of clay. She has a handful of dark, greasy cloth. She pulls again and steps back and more of it slides out.

Boots appear, then legs, a mac that's sopping and daubed in mud, a hood that's pulled down low over a wiry beard.

She picks up her spade and stands there for a long time. She looks down at the pipe, at the new channels cut into the bank, and the water pouring out across her land. She looks down at him. There are three deep spade marks – one in the top of his head, one in his chest, one in his thigh. His skin is as waxy as when you dig up a potato. He's sodden and cold and his teeth are gritted in his jaw, almost, maybe, as if he's grinning up at her.

Well, that's what she says happened anyway.

149

A Year of Buryings

January

The first was Lily Ennis and she did not go peacefully. It was just as the old year slipped into the new one and she clung on, gripping the chair. She'd always thought that the next year would be different – her son would phone, people would visit, someone would beg her to stop smoking. After all, it wasn't up to her to do everything, was it? She clung on. She waited. She's still waiting, actually. When the phone rings, there's a dry intake of breath. In the mornings, there are dents in the arms of the chair.

Next was Riley – sometimes, out of the corner of your eye, you might see him wandering around, talking to himself, wringing his hands. Maybe it's because of the things he did, or maybe it's because of the things he didn't. There he goes now, with his head down, hurrying past.

It's hard to keep track sometimes, what with all the comings, what with all the goings. Every bloody year it's like this – everything changing, everything staying the same.

Violet always swore she'd be kinder.

Lenny always said he'd fix that loose rung on his ladder.

Selwyn made a thousand resolutions. He was going to see an iceberg. He was going to settle down. He would never be late again. You can see his car on its side in the hedge. In spring, it gets covered over when the leaves grow thick. In winter, it shows through again. Thistles are growing in the tyres. There's a bird's nest in the exhaust.

And then there was that man at the crossroads, what was his name? He didn't make any resolutions at all. For him it was better if nothing changed. He'd fallen in love once and look how that turned out. One year blurred into the next, keeping himself to himself, following his own strange routines. He lived by the bus shelter (there's no buses, the timetable's ten years old; there's just a mouldy armchair someone dragged in to help with the waiting). Every year the nettles come up, every year they die back down. He was keeled over in the verge for a month up there before anyone found him. He was up there for a month listening to a badger scratching up his bones.

February

That's the thing – there's a constant shifting of earth round here. It's hard to keep track of it. Bulldozers, cement lorries, gardens ripped out for parking. Houses go up, houses come down. I'm supposed to be remembering, I'm supposed to be getting it all down, but all I can hear is digging and hammering.

Now someone's tapping on windows. Who is it? It's Jameson with his stick, out in the rain again, trying to remember where he used to live.

Wanda tried not to remember. She lay in bed listening to the young people speeding along the top road, doing two-wheelers round the bends. She'd done it herself a long time ago. She'd clipped someone in the dark. God, who was it? She hadn't stopped. She hadn't told anyone. The beat of the engines kept her awake all night. Finally she got up and climbed out of the window. She stood in the road with her arm raised to slow them down. The headlights passed straight through her.

Bradley gritted his teeth and swerved. He crawled out of the windscreen without looking back. He was only nineteen. Now he hangs around on empty farms and outside pubs. No one wants to be the one to say it, but things haven't turned out too differently for him after all.

It turned out Acer had a flair for making enemies.

It turned out everyone was a little bit in love with Annie.

Franklin, meanwhile, died of heartbreak. Don't let anyone try to tell you it was a stroke, or angina. He had all the years mapped out, and then he woke up and his girlfriend's shoes had gone, and her coat, and that suitcase she'd been keeping under the bed. He wrote letters and phoned her about a hundred times a day. He hung around outside her house until they made him stop. There's a holly tree growing out of him now. It's already covered in dark berries. When you walk past it reaches out and tries to snag your clothes.

In the next row across, there's a couple who'd been married over seventy years. They were buried side by side, as close as it was possible to get. If you look carefully you might see a gap appearing, hardly anything, a millimetre, then another millimetre – the kind of thing the gravedigger, a man of geography, would put down to shifting bedrock, or the damn moles, or one of those sinkholes that may one day open up and swallow everything.

March

The cliffs crumbled. A pockmark eroded into a crack, the crack widened until a small overhang broke off and shattered on the beach, exposing smooth shale underneath; the disgruntled fossil of something that remembered better days, when this place was a vast lake next to a mountain range. No one really noticed.

No one noticed the woman going in for a swim either. It was the last day of her holiday and she had that not-quite-left, not-quite-here-any-more feeling. Her bags were packed in the car. The cleaner was sweeping her away. The rip took her out almost to Lundy.

It finally gave back Mr Edwards, though, about forty years too late. There he is in the shallows – washing in and out, thin as a strand of kelp, practically see-through actually. Not a kind man. No one wants to be the one to say it. But maybe a changed man, what with the way the water has smoothed out his bones, the way those barnacles have found the gaps between his fingers.

When Jamie Silver washed off his boat in a storm he made sure he wouldn't be found. He was a claustrophobic man – he didn't want a wooden box, or the hard, packed earth. He'd survived a war and three divorces. Someone had once hit him in the dark with their car. He knew the currents very well; he knew the deepest channels and the rocks he could snag on to. He knew how far he needed to go so that no one could bring him in, or fix him down, or say his life had been this or his life had been that. As far as he was concerned people could look, the meddling, good-hearted bastards, but thank God they'd never find him.

April

In April there was no one.

A dolphin was stranded on the stones. There was no one around apart from the fossil and the fossil didn't give a shit. It had seen it all before. The dolphin started drying out. It forgot what being a dolphin was, until the tide came back in and it swam away and remembered.

A gun went off but I don't think anything's come of it yet.

Someone else came down to retire but I don't think anything's come of that yet either.

It's hard to keep track though. Another supermarket went up practically overnight. Someone built a house in their back garden. The mud got churned, there was nowhere for the rain to go. The last lumps of snow melted and mixed with the soil to create a sort of slush – not liquid exactly, not exactly solid ground.

Lyn slipped into the river on her way home at night. Water poured into her shoes. It was very dark, very cold, and something heavy came down, like a lid closing over her. But she knew she'd get out. She'd had her palm read once and they'd said that her life would be full of tall, exciting men, and she hadn't met any of them yet.

Lenny's nephew almost used the same bloody ladder.

Yardley woke up during his funeral, banging etc.

No one knows what's happened to Lonnie.

Lizzie Wheeler found out about the radioactive properties of granite. How the radon leaked out every day, every minute. How it was odourless and colourless. She started seeing clouds of gas hanging in the air. When she found a lump in her side, nestled under her ribs, she knew exactly what it was. The doctor referred her to the hospital for tests. She felt the lump every day, got to know its precise dimensions, its peculiar firmness. Then, one day, it disappeared. Reabsorbed, the doctor said, shaking her head. On her way home, Lizzie saw a cloud of gas right in front of her. She shivered and walked the long way around it.

And did you hear about Pinky Rowe, who walked unscathed in that lightning storm, carrying a metal umbrella?

May

In May the rain came. You know the kind – warmish, dampish, turning everything into pulpy paper. There's nowhere to go in rain like that. Nothing to do. You suddenly realise the long distances. There aren't many trees to hide under.

In Mikey's house they found washing stolen off the neighbour's line – socks, a nightie, three soft pillowcases.

In Sal's there was a mace under the bed.

June

Someone's watching out of that window. There's a face, too blurry to properly see. It's sort of mottled, sort of furtive-looking. Whoever it is they're just standing there, watching, listening, even though someone's come in and taken away the furniture, even though the curtains are down and the electricity's been switched off. Look – their face is pressed right up to the glass, even though the carpets have been rolled, even though someone's taken away the plates, and the chairs, and letters are banking up on the floor.

Ira didn't take any notice of anyone. Other people and their troubles dripped off him like rain from a waterproof coat. No one's judging – it would probably be blissful really, to not hear things, to not know things. Apart from the fact that he missed what everyone was saying about the eroding cliff path, but there are swings, aren't there, and there are roundabouts.

Look, there goes Maurice again, circling the fields, ripping up handfuls of daisies. He does that every day without stopping. See the way he's rushing, see the way his hands are shaking. It makes you think he must have done something terrible, the way he leaves flowers like that shoved under his wife's door.

Leslie empties a bottle of Scotch every week on the ground where her father's buried. The one time she forgot the grass withered up and turned as dry as ashes.

Which reminds me of something – what is it? Why's it always up to me to remember everything?

That's it. Mrs Edwards is still in the glove compartment of her daughter's car, bumping softly every time it turns. She's waiting to be let go of, waiting, finally, for when there'll be no one orbiting around her like strange, lost planets.

Whereas someone who shall not be named (that old lech) has been shoved unceremoniously, and for all time, into the back of a cupboard.

We should spare a thought for Fuller too, shouldn't we, who never got around to arranging his affairs. He always thought he had more time. He could have been scattered over the water, drifting with the seagulls, being pulled in all directions by the wind. Instead he's on two different mantelpieces in hot front rooms, getting polished every day. It's not so bad actually, except for the way the clocks tick slightly out of sync.

July

The rain turned into a heatwave overnight. The sand roasted. Mud dried for the first time in years. A gorse fire broke out. There was a landslip and the fossil fell onto the beach and was covered over again by stones, just as it had started to get used to things.

Jack Gilbert and Mitch Mitchell were old enemies. Neither of them could remember why. Their farms shared a border and they let out each other's animals and lit dirty bonfires. So when smoke came up from Mitch's place, Jack didn't do anything about it. He went back to his house and watched from the window. The smoke thickened and hung in the air. It didn't smell like one of his normal bonfires – it smelled like there was petrol in it. Mitch had probably left an old can lying around in the yard. He was, and always had been, a complacent man. Jack went to bed. He woke up the next morning with the taste of smoke in his mouth. It was in his hair and his clothes and now, according to him, it won't come out.

Someone got stabbed with a kitchen knife. Someone else got poisoned or something. My God, it's not like the old days round here is it; it's not like those times you could keep your door unlocked. What with people wandering around with blood in their mouths and did you hear that shouting, that choking? I'm just saying.

Two sisters lived in flats one above the other. The smallest noises set them off. They heard each other's TVs. They heard curtains opening and scraping across their runners. They heard each other's breathing and the sounds they made when they were eating. The sister upstairs banged her feet on the floor. The sister downstairs climbed a ladder and banged with her hands. Their hearts went on practically the same day, but they're still doing it – banging and cursing – and neither will be the one that stops first.

There was that woman who put a curse on her mother-in-law, wasn't there? Of course, no one can prove it.

No one can prove who started the rift between the Randalls either. They're a big, sprawling family and even they keep forgetting who's aligned with who. There are cousins who don't speak to cousins, aunts who don't speak to nieces. The grandfather can't go to the cinema any more because his grandson works there, even though he used to love the maroon seats, the musty smell of popcorn. One of the nephews was tiling his roof early in the morning, before the heat set in, when he fell off. There was no one around except his uncle, who was in the next field. The nephew didn't shout to him for help. He couldn't bring himself to do it. If only he'd just shouted. But you know what these things are like between families, don't you – the way they're deep and gleaming, like tin lodes.

August

Here are the last words of Yana: Can somebody …?

Here are the last words of Fletcher: Can anybody …?

No one heard the last words of Dina.

September

The cliffs down the coastline go like this: Mussel Rock, Pigsback Rock, Squench Rock, Cow and Calf, Tense Rocks. The sea chips away at them bit by bit.

A twelve-year-old boy called Rowan fell. His friends called him Yo-Yo. He tried to jump the gap that split a headland into two jutting points. He was wearing a red jumper and the red moved slowly down through the last dried pinks of the thrift and the heather. A group of oystercatchers went up like flares.

In their condolences everyone said he was too young, too full of potential. But the boy's father, stunned and silent, couldn't stop thinking of the boy's wildness: he'd run away from home when he was eight, at ten had broken both wrists falling off a stolen quad. He remembered the hot night back in July when he saw the boy slip into his room, red-eyed and reeking of petrol. That's when he should have done something, that's when he should have stepped in. 'But there was no proof,' he murmured along to the eulogy. After the service, people kept

162

asking why they could smell petrol in the church; did someone's car have a leak that needed seeing to?

Daisy could see herself lying in hospital (she was somewhere at the back, towards the ceiling). Look at all the flowers and cards they'd given her. Listen to the nice things they were saying about her. She shook her head and tried to speak, to correct them – they didn't know about the time she'd left her ailing, fractious mother in a room alone all day, did they? Or the twenty pounds she'd taken from that collection bucket, or how, when her daughter was four and wouldn't stop biting, she'd bitten her right back.

Deano was noted for his wit. You should have seen his impressions. Everyone wanted to stand behind him in a queue; it made the time go so much quicker, it made the day a little bit easier. No one knew that every morning he had to roll his loneliness, his disappointments, down to his feet and step out of them, like a layer of old skin.

For Iris they sang 'Abide With Me' when she'd expected 'Ain't No Sunshine'.

For Peter they bought lilies, forgetting about his allergies.

Only five people came to Radley's – since then he's been passing through walls, knocking on doors, trying to make sure that no one forgets him.

No one's forgotten Greta. She married all three of the Randall brothers and once beat Lonnie in an arm-wrestling match. She had a kind word for everyone, even if it was just the drink talking.

Clement, on the other hand, was an arsehole.

October

More houses went up. More gardens were ripped out for parking. It's endless round here, isn't it? There's a constant shifting of absolutely bloody everything.

A boot washed up on the town beach. People said it was Jamie Silver's. There was the mark of his needle and thread at the soles – no one else in town repaired their own shoes.

A hand washed up as well, but how am I meant to know who that belongs to?

Selma Richards left her body at the bottom of the stairs and got up feeling so much lighter. That thing had always been a burden, what with its aches and its twinges, its cracked veins and its dry skin, its ridged nails and its gammy eyes, its stiff hips and its dropped arches, its swollen glands and its knotty hair and its wisdom teeth only ever half coming through.

Giles left a house full of things he couldn't throw away – damp newspapers, tins, plastic bottles. It was stacked up to the ceilings. He had his own elaborate systems. If you squint you might see him over there in the corner, slowly reordering it, folding bags, flattening cardboard boxes, dust in his hair, dust on his clothes. When he was nine, he'd thrown away his favourite toy – a bear with warm, coppery fur – because someone said he was too old for it. He'd looked for it for days but never found it.

There were a few more sloes, a few less people. The cliffs turned almost burgundy. Geese flew over, creaking like trains. There was one tangled in the weeds by the road, well, just its feathers – the whole thing sort of broken open the way a thistle-head opens.

Dooley, the thatcher, left his signature twist of straw in every roof in the area.

Gregory left nothing worth mentioning.

Myrtle left five sons, twelve grandchildren, eighteen great-grandchildren: a whole bloody dynasty.

November

Pinky Rowe went out in the lightning again. No one wants to be the one to say it, but people never really learn do they.

Farley, for example, never learned to say no to anything.

Hazel never gave up those burnt bits – the black edges of toast, the dark crackling, the scrapings at the side of the pot. The doctor said they'd take five years off her. It was probably worth it.

December

The problem is, there's always too much happening. There's one thing and then there's always another. How am I supposed to get it all down, what am I supposed to say exactly?

I could tell you, I suppose, that Kenny's last thought was the sound of the leaves on the poplar tree in his first garden.

And the last thought of Ikey involved that bright sauce from the Chinese takeaway. (He wished it had been something more highfalutin.)

Or maybe I should say that Vanda wished for one more kiss of the lobe of her husband's ear.

Or that Opal's wish was so small, so secret, that no one could hear?

Then there's Davey, who could have.

And Bunny, who should have.

And what about Floyd, who'd done everything he wanted? When he'd worked at the pub on the cliffs collecting empty glasses, he held the record for a stack of fifty. He'd given money to charity, been a godfather to a baby. He'd stroked a tiger at the carnival, had witnessed a glittering sweep of phosphorescence out across the water. And once, he'd caught the cleanest wave at Salthouse and ridden it right in, the dark green of it arching beautifully, smoothly, behind his back.

What the hell am I meant to do with that?

Thank God the year's almost ending. Although that just means there's another one coming.

It's hard to keep track, what with all the comings, what with all the goings. And I suppose it's up to me to see what happens next, is it? The cliffs are still crumbling, the fossil's getting buried deeper in the stones. Houses are still going up. Houses are still coming down. All that earth's still shifting around. Every bloody year it's like this – everything changing, everything staying the same.

Cables

'THERE'S THOSE HOLES AGAIN,' Morrie says. He leans back against the bench and puts his hands in his coat pockets.

'They weren't there yesterday,' Fran says. She watches a gull that is watching her. The concrete under the bench is sandy. There are bits of dry seaweed and cigarette butts that roll in the wind.

'It must have happened in the night.'

'That's when it usually happens.'

A woman walks towards them speaking into a phone. They stop talking and tilt their heads until she's gone past.

'There's a lot of them this time,' Morrie says. 'They're right across the beach.'

'Down to the water.'

'The sand's been flung everywhere.'

'Look how deep that one is.'

'Look how deep that one is.'

'You could climb a ladder down that one.'

Their eyes follow the holes across the sand.

'Apparently there's a pattern,' Morrie says.

'Is there?'

'That's what I heard.'

'Who said that?'

'I heard it.'

'What pattern?'

'It's systematic.'

They look from left to right along the sand, then from the top of the beach to the bottom. The gull edges closer and Fran claps her hands. The gull stops, but still watches them.

'The tide will come in soon,' Morrie says. 'It'll cover them over.'

'It's halfway in now.'

They look out at the sea. Small waves surge. There is a deeper, darker line of water where a current moves. The shadows of clouds skim across like boats.

Morrie sighs and rests his hands on his stomach. 'Then he'll come back with his spade and dig more.'

Fran zips her coat up tighter. 'That's what he always does.'

'Listening.'

'Digging.'

'Listening.'

The waves break then drag back across the stones. The stones clatter as they turn.

'He didn't always hear it,' Morrie says. 'He was just going along, doing what he always did.'

170

'Listening.'

'Finding things out.'

'He knew everything around here.'

'About everyone.'

'You couldn't tell him anything – he'd already heard it.'

'Who stole that statue.'

'What happened to Lonnie.'

They fold their arms and hunch against the wind.

'He had to know everything,' Morrie says.

'He did.'

'He always had to know more.'

'He did.'

'Then he started thinking about the cables.' Morrie leans back and stretches out his legs. 'How they come in under the beach. How they're passing by, right under his feet. With all that information. All those communications.'

'I heard it's telephone calls.'

'I heard it's emails.'

'Financial transactions.'

'The stock exchange.'

'Internet searches.'

'Messages.'

'All of it.'

'Everything.'

'Right here, under the sand.'

They look out across the beach. The gull takes a few running steps forward, then stops and sidles back.

'He couldn't stop thinking about it all.'

'He wouldn't stop thinking about it all.'

'Coming in every minute.'

'Every second.'

'Then, one day, he heard buzzing.'

'It was only faint at first.'

'He hardly noticed it,' Morrie says. 'He told himself it was just a fly, or machinery in the distance.'

'Like when someone's vacuuming in another house up the street.'

'Or you walk past the tattoo place.'

'Or when a bulb's about to go.'

'It was faint. But it carried on. After three days he went and got checked. He thought it could be something inside his ears.'

'Maybe it was.'

'They said there was nothing wrong.'

'Maybe there wasn't.'

'But then it started getting louder.'

'How loud?'

'Like a lawnmower.'

'I'd have said a Strimmer.'

'He started hearing it every day. It would suddenly start up when he was at the pub, and he'd glance around, seeing if anyone else could hear it. He'd shake his head and rub over the top of his jaw. Gradually it would fade and he'd tell himself he was imagining it. Then, later, when he was walking down the street, he'd notice it again.'

'What about at work?'

'I heard he doesn't work any more.'

They stop and their heads slowly tilt. Two people walk past talking quietly to each other.

Fran looks back at the road. There is sand, fields, a few scattered houses. 'He lives somewhere up there, doesn't he?'

'He does now.'

'By himself?'

'He is now.'

Fran sighs and shakes her head. The gull walks a bit closer, then stops just out of reach of their feet. It stares at something.

'He couldn't sleep. He stopped reading the paper. He stopped watching TV. You'd be trying to have a conversation with him and he'd just be staring out towards the beach.'

'I wouldn't like that,' Fran says.

'He put earplugs in. He walked around with his hands over his ears. It helped at first, but then the noise changed.'

'How did it change?'

'It got closer. It was very close, like it was inside the ear itself. It was more high-pitched, a sort of rushing sound.'

'Constant?'

'All the time.'

Fran sighs again. The tide presses in. Water and sand pour into one of the holes. When the wave pulls back, the hole is full and level again with the beach.

'I heard he's got maps,' Morrie says. 'Where he thinks they come in. The different beaches. Working out where to dig. How to get to them.'

'Who said that?'

'I heard it.'

'They must be deep.'

'They've got to be deep, cables like that.'

'And he reckons he can hear them?'

They lean forward slowly. There is the wind and the low beat of the waves. The bench creaks under them.

'I can't hear them,' Fran says.

Morrie leans further forward. 'I don't know if I just heard something.'

'What?'

'I don't know. Something.'

Fran tilts her head and frowns. 'Maybe I heard something too.'

'What?'

They listen. The sand blows lightly over their feet. The gull scrapes one of its claws against the concrete and tenses.

'What if you did start thinking about it?' Fran says.

'All of it.'

'Everything.'

'Passing you by.'

'Every minute.'

'Every second.'

They glance at each other, then sit upright on the bench. The gull rushes forward, grabs a cold chip from between Fran's feet and flies away.

Morrie leans back. 'I don't think I can hear it any more.'

'Neither can I.'

They watch the tide fill in another hole. The waves break then drag back against the stones. The stones clatter as they turn.

Morrie shifts again on the bench. 'Did you hear about what happened with those neighbours?'

'The ones with the ditch?'

'The ones with the ditch.'

Fran reaches down and brushes the sand off her shoes. 'I might have heard something about it,' she says.

The Sing of the Shore

HE'D BEEN DRIVING ALL day and his eyes were dry, his shoulders cracking like pipes. Three hours, maybe four, that's how long he'd thought it would take, but he'd been driving for over eight. The roads had narrowed the closer he got, and now they were single track, with clumps of grass down the middle and flanked by bulky hedges. Beyond them were ridged fields, pylons, a few barns with collapsed roofs, the wet wind dousing everything.

The road turned stony. Potholes made the car jump. The road narrowed again and Bryce stopped, tried to see where he was, then kept going. He was sure he'd missed it. Nothing around here looked exactly as he remembered – that farmhouse wasn't there before, was it? And that dark mass of trees? He stopped again and got out. Daffodils lit the bank like torches. He climbed up and looked over, could just glimpse the sea at the bottom of the fields. He stood there for a long time. There was the same old wind above and the same old waves below, knuckling together like they were shaping loaves of bread.

He drove forward again, then stopped suddenly at a gate, which was open and hanging off its hinges. He turned in and parked on the long grass. There were the campsite's corrugated huts – the kitchen, the laundry, the shower block. There was the office – a caravan at the bottom of the slope – and the swing; but it was all rusted out, overgrown, and one of the swing's chains had snapped. There was no one around. It was early spring and there should have been people staying by now; the fields scattered with tents and campfires, the roar of gas from stoves.

He took his bag out and crossed over to the bungalow to find Kensa. Skylarks rose up from the grass, their songs tangling together. He could smell clover, gorse, the mucky, shitty smell from the next field over. A tractor was ploughing in the distance, gulls following behind like a reel of cotton unspooling.

He was almost at the house when he looked up and saw a woman standing in the window, talking on a phone. He was about to wave then stopped, almost stumbling in the furrowed mud. It wasn't his sister. He turned and scanned the fields, then turned back to the house. The woman was staring at him and pointing at something over his shoulder. It took him a moment to realise that she meant the caravan. He nodded, pulled his bag higher onto his shoulder, and made his way down the slope.

There was a low sound coming from somewhere – almost too low to notice. The further down the field he went, the louder it got. It was a sort of booming. He stopped and looked around, but couldn't see anything. It wasn't the waves; he could hear those breaking slowly against the rocks. This was deeper, more like an echo, or a murmur behind a wall. He kept going through the long grass. After a while he told himself he couldn't hear it any more.

The caravan's door was shut and there were curtains across the windows. He went up the step and knocked. He waited a moment then knocked again, and when there was no answer he pushed gently on the door. Inside, the room was cramped and stale. He was expecting the desk and the swivel chair, but there was also a mattress on the floor with a blanket on it he recognised. There was a gas heater, and a pan on the hob. Kensa must have rigged the caravan up to the mains because the fridge under the sink was humming and there was a dim lamp in the corner.

He put his bag down and went over to the desk. All the office stuff was there – the money box, the check-in forms, the accounts book. He opened the accounts and looked at the figures. They were low. No one had stayed over the winter; hardly anyone the summer before. There were no bookings for the months coming up either.

There was a noise outside and suddenly Kensa was in the doorway. They stared at each other for a moment, then she came in, sat on the mattress and started pulling off her boots. 'You're back then,' she said.

Bryce closed the book. 'You sold the house,' he said. He moved away from the desk and knocked into a box of clothes. He pulled out the chair and sat in it, rubbing his fingers into the corners of his eyes. When their parents died, Kensa had taken over the place. Bryce had already gone. He remembered the day she'd moved back into the bungalow – it was the last time he'd been here.

'I saved your share,' Kensa said. 'Of the money.' She got up, opened one of the cupboards, closed it, then opened it again. She brought out a few tins, emptied one into the pan and lit the flame. 'Are you hungry?' She seemed smaller somehow; there was a stoop to the top of her back. She kept running her hand through her hair, which she'd cut short. There were the same three hoops in each ear. She was past forty; he could hardly believe it, Christ, he was almost forty himself. He felt too big for the space – he was suddenly aware of how bulky he'd let his waist get, the extra weight around his hips. There was still the same wiriness about Kensa, or maybe rigidity, like she was holding herself away from something.

'I just need a few days,' he said, gesturing to his bag. 'Maybe a week.' There was nowhere else he could go. A few things hadn't worked out, a few things needed waiting out, and then they'd be OK again, like a piece of glass battered into smoothness by time and the sea.

Kensa stirred the pan. 'Are beans alright?' she asked.

She'd never liked beans, and neither had Bryce. It was the way the skins peeled off and crumbled. As kids they'd gone round to an aunt's for dinner and fed them to the dog under the table.

He leaned back in the chair and it cracked softly. 'Yeah,' he said. 'Sounds good.'

~

Summers on the campsite were long and empty. There was nothing nearby – no shop, no park, no other houses. Their parents were too busy to take them anywhere so Bryce and Kensa would hang around by the kitchen block, light matches from the spare box, bet which tent would collapse first, or who would trip over a guy rope. They went through the left-behind clothes in the laundry and put on whatever they found. Sometimes Kensa wore rolled-up overalls; sometimes a velvet dress which slipped off her shoulders. Bryce wore a Hawaiian shirt that smelled of aftershave.

At first, they made friends with other kids who came to stay – there was that girl with the head-brace, and that boy who could burp the alphabet – but after a while Kensa decided they wouldn't do it any more. They didn't need anyone else. The other kids always left. They never turned round to wave from the backseats of their cars; they probably forgot about them as soon as they went past the gate. All that would be left were the yellow squares of grass where their tents had been, and a few charred sticks from their fires.

Instead, Kensa stole bright soaps from the showers and chocolate out of the communal fridge. At night, they would crouch by the tents, listening. Sometimes there would be arguing, sometimes singing. Sometimes there would be strange noises in there that Bryce didn't recognise, and Kensa would put her hands over his ears.

She could hold her breath until her lips went grey, and throw the peeling knife into the door so hard that it quivered. She would push back her stringy fringe and stare out at things Bryce couldn't see. Once, she found a chunk of ice on the grass outside the front door. It was about the size of a grapefruit and it was just there suddenly, one day, in the heat. They had no idea where it had come from. She picked it up and kept it in the freezer, behind the bread and the bag of peas. Sometimes they would take it out and look for a long time at the blue-tinged crystals. Bryce followed her everywhere.

They got sunburn, grass rash, nettle stings, bites from mosquitoes and horseflies. Kensa would find dock leaves and spit on Bryce's bites. She picked her own into scars. When a group of boys crushed a patch of strawberries he'd been growing, she went out in the night and undid their guy ropes, so that their tent collapsed on them in the rain.

Then, one summer, Nate came. It was a dark, muggy summer, the kind that always seems to be brewing storms, but no storm ever hits. Flies banged into the windows and lay twitching against the glass. Mushrooms bloomed and disappeared overnight.

Bryce was nine and Kensa was twelve. Nate arrived late one afternoon and set up a small tent in the corner of the field, far away from everyone. He was seventeen. No one knew where he'd come from. He paid by the week and said he didn't know how long he'd be staying. At night, a small torch would shine out from his tent, and stay on until morning.

~

Kensa cleared up the food and put the plates in the sink. She glanced at Bryce, then around the cramped room. 'I guess I should give you the mattress,' she said.

Bryce's eyes were closing and he forced them open. He zipped his jacket up to his chin – he could almost see his breath in front of him. 'Have you still got that tent?' he said. 'The spare one?' They always used to keep a spare in case any of the visitors' tents broke.

'Maybe,' Kensa said. 'I'll go and look.' She put her boots back on and went out into the dark. The wind came in the door and blew the papers across the desk.

Bryce's eyes closed again. He must have slept for a moment because he suddenly jerked awake. He didn't know where he was, and he stood up, took a step forward, felt the small walls pressing in. There was a low noise, deep and almost regular, as if there was too much pressure in his ears. He crossed the room and opened the door, almost walking into Kensa.

'Can you hear that?' Bryce said.

'What?'

'That.' He went down the step and onto the grass.

'The wind's picking up,' Kensa said. She was holding a tent, a sleeping bag and a torch. 'We should put this up.'

Bryce listened again. The wind was thudding against the caravan, making the loose glass in the window clunk. He'd forgotten the way the gales careened over the cliffs like that: head first, with nothing in their way. 'I'll do it,' he said. He went inside and got his bag, then took all the camping stuff from Kensa. 'See you in the morning, OK?'

A bat brushed past his face, then swung low over the grass. Kensa went inside. He could see her through a gap in the curtain – she sat down on the mattress, got up again, took out a bottle of something and poured it into a mug.

Bryce walked down the field until he found a flat pitch to put up the tent. He unpacked it from the bag and shone the torch on the poles and the rusty pegs. The wind dragged the material out of his hands. It was soft and mouldy and there were dead flies studded in the netting.

He put up the buckling poles, spread the canvas over them, then realised it was inside out. He took the canvas off, turned it over, fastened it back down, then hammered in the pegs, hammering his finger by mistake and swearing into the wind. The pegs bent against the stony ground but finally went in.

Kensa's light was still on when he zipped up the door.

He shifted on the ground, turned onto his side, then his back. He pulled the sleeping bag higher, then dropped it back down. He didn't want to know what the smell was in there.

An hour passed, and then another. It started to rain and a few drops splashed onto his legs. He moved over to the other side of the tent. He needed a mat, maybe some cushions. There was a stone jutting into his hip, and another one in his shoulder. He turned over again.

The sky lightened slowly and a chill came up from the ground. Finally he gave up, pulled on a jumper and jeans, found his towel at the bottom of his bag, and went over the wet grass to the shower block. It had been a long time since he'd walked outside with bare feet – he'd forgotten the sponginess of it, the bristle of dandelion leaves, the way daisies snapped off between his toes.

He took a piss then turned on the shower. There were cracks everywhere, clumps of mud and dried grass, brittle spiders that must have died years ago. Red gunk dribbled between the tiles and there were yellow flakes of old soap on the floor.

Whenever he'd imagined Kensa, it hadn't been like this. He'd thought of her walking between bright tents, letting down guy ropes in the night if someone had been a jerk. He'd thought it would all be the same, suspended somehow, like a point on a map, even when Kensa's face became blurred, even when the campsite faded like paint running over wet paper. They hadn't spoken for a long time. He'd meant to phone, to get in touch, but he'd always been moving from place to place, from job to job, always trying to find the next thing, waiting for when he could say, finally, here I am.

The water ran lukewarm, almost cold. He came out shivering.

That summer they would get up early, slipping out before their parents made them do any chores. What they hated was cleaning out the showers, emptying bins, looking for mouldy bread or bottles of green milk in the kitchen. So they disappeared, taking handfuls of dry cereal with them. They weren't meant to go far – beyond the campsite there were cliffs, rips, caves, long drops to gravelly beaches – so they stayed around the lanes and the fields, walking back and forth along the dark hedges. The fields had barley in them, which moved in the wind like muscles under a horse's back. Kensa would get Bryce to hide in the stalks and then she would try to find him. She'd start counting and Bryce would crawl away through the damp soil, his heart pummelling in his throat, trying not to snap any of the stalks and give himself away. Kensa always found him.

One morning he'd been hiding for a long time. He'd found a gap big enough to sit in, and he was waiting, the skin on his hands tingling. Minutes passed, then maybe half an hour. An ant crawled up his leg. It was hot down there and the clouds were getting thick and murky.

'Kensa?' he said quietly. Another ant went up his leg. Voices drifted over the field towards him. He stood up, but he couldn't see anything except the stalks rippling.

He walked towards the voices. One of them sounded like Kensa's but he couldn't tell who the other person was. He crossed the field and came out at the edge, his cheeks dusty, seeds knotted in his hair. It was Kensa and that boy, Nate, from the campsite. They were standing by the gate, talking. It took them a moment to see Bryce.

'Hello there,' Nate said. 'Who are you?'

'That's just Bryce,' Kensa said. 'My brother.'

Bryce brushed another ant off his leg. 'You were meant to find me,' he said.

Kensa picked at a barley stalk. 'This is Nate,' she said. 'Remember?'

'You were supposed to find me,' Bryce told her.

Kensa bent the stalk around her arm and left it there, like a bracelet. 'You were saying about the glow-worms,' she said to Nate.

Nate pushed at his glasses and sniffed. He sounded blocked up. 'I thought I'd go and look for them. There's meant to be a lot round here.' He was short and his face was pale and creased, like a pillow in the morning. He had a shaved head and bare feet.

'Glow-worms?' Bryce said.

'You can come if you want,' Nate said. He spoke quietly, almost with a lisp, which made him sound even more out of breath.

'I'll come,' Kensa said. She wound another stalk round her wrist.

'I was hiding for ages,' Bryce said. The clouds got even darker and a few drops of rain fell onto the dusty ground. He stood there, picking the seeds out of his hair, then he turned and went back into the field, found his hiding place and crouched down, muttering to himself and digging in the soil with his fingers. He didn't come out when Kensa called him.

That evening, Kensa didn't eat all her dinner. She kept some back and put it on another plate in secret. When she went out

of the back door, Bryce followed. She crossed over the main
site and went down to Nate's tent, then sat outside with him
while he ate.

~

Bryce was alone on the campsite. He didn't know where Kensa
had gone. It was late afternoon and just starting to get dark.
He'd spent most of the day reinforcing his tent, patching the
leaks with tape and trying to find a mat to lie on. Now he got a
bucket of water, disinfectant, a cloth, crusty rubber gloves, and
started cleaning the shower block. He turned on all the strip
lights, which buzzed and clanked, then gritted his teeth while
he did the plugholes and the sink and between the tiles. He
washed away the spiders and the strung-up midges, then took
the casing off the lights and tipped out the husks of wasps. He
poured bleach everywhere and came out coughing, his eyes red
around the rims.

He did the same with the laundry room and the kitchen.
He emptied the bins, threw away old socks, swept up onion
skins and peeled desiccated teabags from the floor. He mopped
and threw down more bleach. Then he washed his hands a
thousand times and went down to his tent.

Kensa was back. He knocked at the caravan and went in. She
was sitting at the desk with a book in front of her, squinting in
the dim light.

'I cleaned the blocks,' Bryce said. The bottle of whisky was
out on the sink and he poured some into a mug for himself,

topped up Kensa's, then sat down on the edge of the mattress. 'It doesn't look like many people have been using them.'

Kensa closed the book slowly. Bryce thought he recognised the cover from the pile of left-behind books in the kitchen. It was some kind of musty out-of-date travel guide, the edges yellow and curled. The lamp cast shadows below her eyes.

'When did the last person stay?' he said.

The light flickered and Kensa frowned and tapped the bulb. 'I don't remember.'

Bryce shifted on the mattress. He took a long drink, and then another.

'Other sites have opened up,' she said. 'Around.'

'Maybe you should …'

The bulb flickered again. 'Don't do this now,' Kensa said.

Bryce shifted again on the mattress. The blanket was rucked up under him. He picked it up. It was tiny and fraying, and there was a wobbly K written on the label. He looked around at the bare walls, the boxes of clothes, the bottle of drink. This was what he'd just come from – except that, for him, it was because he was always just on the cusp of leaving.

'Kensa,' he said.

The lamp pinged and snapped off.

'Shit,' Kensa said. The fridge stopped humming. The lights at the edge of the campsite went black and they were plunged into the dark.

Bryce got up and stepped forward, stumbling over Kensa's foot.

'Stay still,' Kensa said. 'I need to find the torch.'

'I'll find it.'

'Just stay still.'

There was the sound of cupboards and drawers opening, and a moment later the torch was on, the door had opened and she was zipping up her coat.

Bryce followed her down the step and onto the grass. The darkness was almost solid – it seemed to press outwards, filling everything like gas expanding to fill a space.

Kensa's voice came from behind him. 'It's the trip switch. I need to re-jig the wires,' she said. 'It always bloody does this.' She started walking over to the kitchen block.

He watched her go. He'd thought, for a moment, that when he'd stumbled in the caravan she was about to say, have a nice trip.

In the distance, the bungalow was still lit up. There was a family in there, sitting round a table, steam rising slowly from their plates.

Kensa spent more and more time with Nate. Instead of waiting for Bryce in the morning, she would leave before he was up, disappearing on long walks out to the cliffs and down to the rocks and the beaches.

When Bryce tried to follow, he always got caught by his parents. When they asked where Kensa was he pursed his lips and said he didn't know. He had to do the chores alone: mopping the floors, smearing the mud around the tiles, wiping

190

the stained mirrors. The coins they gave him afterwards rattled like stones in his pocket.

A family came and set up a big tent with an awning that flapped like a broken wing.

There was a boy who looked about the same age as Bryce, so Bryce went over there and stood by the door until the boy finally came out and started kicking a ball around by himself.

'Kick it to me,' Bryce said.

'Why?'

'Kick it to me.'

The boy kept the ball under his foot so Bryce kicked it away, then picked it up and ran off with it. The boy followed him.

'Let's go and listen at that tent,' Bryce said.

The boy stared at him.

'Let's crouch down behind it and listen.'

'Why?'

Bryce picked a flake of rubber off the ball. It was muddy and wet. 'I don't know.'

The other boy went back into his tent. He didn't come back for the ball.

Bryce went down to the bottom of the campsite and looked out. He could see Kensa and Nate far below, on the rocks. They were just walking. They never did anything except walk and talk quietly about things, their heads bent together. Bryce could never catch what they were saying. He would listen, but their voices would blur and hum, and get tugged away by the wind.

Kensa took Nate bits of food from the fridge and loose change she found down the back of the sofa. She'd told him how to work the washing machine for free. She'd shown him the chunk of ice and Nate had held it up, looked at it for a long time, then said it was probably the remains of something someone had flushed out of a toilet on an aeroplane. After that Kensa didn't take it out any more.

Bryce watched them until they disappeared round the headland, then he started walking back. He passed Nate's tent, and slowed down. A thin sheet of rain was billowing in across the fields. The edges of the clouds were orange, almost smouldering. He looked around, then unzipped the tent and went in.

There was hardly anything in there: a mat, a sleeping bag, a damp towel, a jumper rolled up for a pillow. There was a rucksack by the door and Bryce took everything out and laid it on the ground. There was a book, a torch, a few spare clothes, a pair of fraying socks that had been repaired with neat stitches. Half a bar of chocolate. Allergy tablets. An old bus ticket.

He looked it all over carefully, then put every item back exactly as he'd found it, except he ripped a small corner of the book before closing it.

Bryce was taking his rubbish up to the bins when the woman from the bungalow came out. She was wearing a long, baggy jumper that went past her knees, and rubber gloves which dripped water on the path. A small boy was watching from the window, his hands pushed up against the glass.

'Are you Bryce?' she asked.

Bryce opened the bin and threw his bag in. He nodded.

'We bought the house, a couple of years back?'

'I saw that,' Bryce told her.

The woman glanced over to check on the boy. 'Kensa's talked about you.'

As soon as she'd turned away again, the boy pressed his face against the window, squashing his cheeks and lips into fat white shapes.

'She has?'

The woman pulled at a loose thread on her jumper, but couldn't hold on to it with the rubber gloves. 'We sometimes worry about her, living out in that caravan – we …' She trailed off and pulled again at the thread. 'What I wanted to ask you was, would you both like to come over for dinner later?'

'Dinner?' Bryce said.

'If you're free.'

'Later?' He looked behind him, as if that would determine the answer. He looked at the house – the kitchen, the hallway. That kid was probably sleeping in his old room. He rubbed a finger over his eye. 'We're actually busy tonight,' he said. 'Sorry about that.'

He waited for her to suggest another night, but she didn't. She just shrugged and smiled and said that it was OK.

He went back and told Kensa.

'Bollocks,' she said. 'Now we have to go somewhere.'

'Where can we go?'

'There isn't anywhere.'

'We have to go somewhere.' He glanced outside, saw the grass, the swing, his tent buckling in the wind. 'We'll drive to the pub.'

'It closed.'

'Bollocks.'

Kensa took two mugs out of the cupboard and sat down. 'We'll have to stay in here with all the lights off.'

'We're not doing that.'

'Why?'

Bryce went out of the caravan, scanned the fields, his car, then went up to the blocks. He paced around the kitchen. There was a pile of old driftwood in the corner, and a box of matches. He carried it all back down to the caravan, then found some tins of food, bread, a few cans of beer. 'Come on,' he said.

They crossed the fields and took the path that sloped down the cliff. There was a ledge, and then another, lower ledge – a wide outcrop ringed with thrift, which trembled in the wind. The sea was still far below them, the tops of the waves cutting across like torn edges of paper. A flock of gulls glided out towards the deeper water.

Bryce piled the wood up, rolled some newspaper and lit it. The wind blew the flame straight out. He tried again, shielding it with his back.

'Let me try,' Kensa said. She crouched down and blew into the middle of the wood. A flame sputtered and spread and a line of smoke twisted out.

Bryce rested the tins on the fire and soon they were scalding. They waited for them to cool, then pulled up the lids and ate, scooping out meatballs and folding them into bread, drinking the dregs of sauce at the bottom. The driftwood spat out salt into the dark.

Kensa sat forwards with her arms wrapped around her knees. Her head was slightly to one side, as if she was listening for something. She'd gone out again all that morning; he didn't know where she went, what she did all day. Bryce started to speak, stopped, shifted on the stones. Sparks spat and went out.

'When do you think we can go back up?' he said.

Kensa watched the fire. She opened the beers and passed one over to him. 'Not yet,' she said. She settled back against a rock.

Bryce threw another bit of wood on the fire. Smoke billowed like a sheet. It crossed his mind that Kensa had probably sat in the caravan with all the lights off before, to avoid other invitations.

'Remember when you almost stabbed yourself with that knife?' Kensa said.

Bryce looked up. 'I thought it was that fake one.'

'It wasn't the fake one,' Kensa said.

'Where the blade slid into the handle.'

'It wasn't the fake one.'

'I'd started pushing it into my stomach.'

'I had to knock it out of your hand.'

They drank their beers and watched the fire. Minutes passed, or maybe hours. Bryce could still feel the sharp point of the knife – there was a scar there somewhere, below his belly button, hidden now by a line of wiry hair.

'Do you remember Nate?' he asked suddenly.

'What?'

'Nate, that guy who stayed here on his own, do you remember him?'

Kensa put her can down slowly. The fire was almost out. She got up and stood on a rock, looking over towards the campsite. 'It's probably safe to go back up now.' She used her boot to scrape ash over the last few embers.

~

Bryce's bedroom was small and tidy. It had a desk and a globe and his shoes were lined up by the door. There was a stain on the carpet in the corner, which he'd covered with a cushion, from when he and Kensa had mixed together baking powder and vinegar to make a bomb, but it had gone off too quickly. He could still smell the vinegar on hot mornings.

He was just getting up – the long, empty day stretching ahead of him – when Kensa flung the door open, knocking over the globe. She was breathing hard, and her shoes and legs were flecked with wet grass.

'He's gone,' she said.

Bryce folded the top of his duvet down carefully.

'Did you hear what I said? Nate's gone.'

'What do you mean gone?'

'I went out there and he's gone.'

Bryce smoothed the duvet, then straightened and smoothed his pillow.

'His tent's there,' Kensa said. 'But none of his stuff. His bag's gone.' She was pacing the room now. The tops of her cheeks had gone very pale, almost white. 'I told Mum and Dad but they're not worried at all. They said he'd paid up yesterday and must have moved on. I said what about his tent, he wouldn't leave his tent, and they said it was a crummy old tent and people leave crummy tents all the time. They were annoyed because now they have to take it down and get rid of it themselves.' She paced over to the window and looked out. 'Say something.'

'He just left,' Bryce told her.

'But he didn't say he was going,' Kensa said. 'He wasn't meant to go.'

Bryce went over to the window and stood next to her. He scratched at the paint on the frame. 'Let's go and hide in the field,' he said. The day suddenly seemed not so long, not so empty. 'Let's go,' he said.

Kensa stayed by the window.

It was late morning and Bryce came down from the kitchen eating a handful of dry cereal and drinking from a mug of thick black coffee. He knocked on the caravan and waited for Kensa. He was going out to buy food and wanted to know if she needed anything.

He knocked again, then went in. Kensa had already gone. There was a bowl and mug in the sink and a pan on the hob, which was still warm when he touched it. He went outside and stood on the step, thought he just caught a glimpse of her walking across the field. He closed the door, turned, and followed her.

He took the same paths they used to take, past the edges of the fields, where the barley was only just starting to come up. When he used to crawl through the stalks, the fields had seemed vast, stretching for miles in all directions, the rows like corridors that never ended, but now he crossed them in a moment, remembering the feeling of warm dust on his cheeks, the scratchy earth under his knees. He almost heard the sound of Kensa counting down, almost felt the old fearful tingle that meant she'd got to zero.

He climbed the gate and turned towards the headland. The wind had dropped overnight and the air was warmer, denser. The clouds had a dark tinge to them, like damp behind a wall. The path edged down and he scanned the rocks below. The tide was in and the sea was gnashing at them, the white water roiling like a cauldron.

He pushed on further. His knees ached and his T-shirt was sticking to his skin. He should have caught up with her by now, or at least be able to see her somewhere further along the path.

He skidded on a gritty slope and stopped. He looked around again. There was nothing, no one, just a buzzard keening overhead, a swathe of blue flowers like stitches in the grass, and then the low, dull booming, so low he almost couldn't hear it, echoing across the rocks, the sea, the sky, as if it was coming from everywhere.

~

Sometimes, when their parents had to go away for the day, Bryce and Kensa would be in charge of the office, answering the phone and taking down bookings. There was a pile of forms and pens, and an old chipped phone. The caravan was cool and musty. Thin spiders hung in the corners. There was a new chair in there that swivelled and Kensa sat on it behind the desk. Bryce sat at the top of the step, in a wedge of sun that came in the doorway. Clouds moved across and the caravan went from dark to light, dark to light, until the skin on his arms turned to goosebumps.

Kensa spun slowly in the chair, staring out of the window. The phone rang but she didn't move.

'You have to answer that,' Bryce said.

'You do it.'

'It's your turn.' They always took it in turns. Bryce hated answering the phone. He could never remember how much they charged each night, or if they had electric hook-ups. The voices on the other end sounded impatient and far away. They asked him how old he was and where his parents were. Sometimes Kensa answered all the calls. She would use a funny accent and make him almost retch with laughing.

Bryce watched the phone. Eventually it stopped ringing.

Kensa was still looking out of the window. 'He wouldn't have left his tent,' she said. 'If he didn't have his tent, where would he sleep? He didn't have anywhere else to go. He didn't have anyone.'

'We should have taken that booking,' Bryce told her.

Kensa spun the chair back towards the desk. She opened the bookings folder and flipped back through the pages, running her finger down the columns. 'Here's where he checked in,' she said. 'And here …' She looked closer. 'See, he didn't actually check out.'

'He paid the full amount,' Bryce said.

'He didn't officially check out.'

The phone rang again but Kensa didn't look up.

Bryce's throat felt dry. It wasn't his turn. What was he meant to say? Hello, you're through to bookings? How can I help you? Welcome to …

Kensa didn't move. The phone kept ringing. Bryce picked it up and held it to his ear, and forgot to say anything at all.

~

A car drove into the campsite and a woman got out. She was about fifty, and she was wearing wellies and a leather jacket. There were a lot of silver bracelets on one of her wrists. She stood by the car for a moment, looking round at the site, then started walking down to the office.

Bryce had been washing the outside of the caravan, which was coated in a rind of mildew. The car's radio was blaring as it came in and he recognised the song but couldn't place it – the music sounded strange, too loud, like something half-familiar from a long time ago. He put the cloth down and dried his hands.

The woman nodded at him, and looked around again at the site, following the slope of grass up to the blocks, down to the sea.

'It's warming up,' Bryce said. He went inside and found a check-in form and a pen. He knew that, eventually, people would start coming. 'We've got a lot of flat pitches. How big's your tent?'

'I don't have a tent,' the woman said.

'Are you bringing a caravan?'

'I'm not staying.' She put her hand up as if to shield her eyes against a glare, even though it wasn't bright. Her bracelets jangled. 'I'm actually here to …'

Just then Kensa came back from the laundry room carrying a bag of washing. When she saw the woman she frowned and shook her head.

'You said you'd think about it again,' the woman said.

Kensa went inside with the washing, slammed a cupboard, then came back out. She took the cloth out of Bryce's bucket and started thumping it against the caravan. Soap ran down the metal and onto the grass. 'I told you last time,' she said.

'I'm offering good money,' the woman said. 'Take it off your hands. Like I said, I'd do the place up, look after it.'

Kensa scrubbed hard at a thick patch of green. She plunged the cloth in the bucket and slopped it out again. The water turned grey.

'You're living in the office,' the woman said.

'I told you already.'

The woman glanced at Bryce, then took one more look over the site. Her hair kept blowing across her face. She pushed it back behind her ears, holding the rest in her hand. A few staticky strands lifted, as if a balloon had been rubbed over it. 'I'll come back in a few weeks,' she said. 'Give you some more time.' She looked once more at Bryce, then started walking back to her car. A daisy she'd stepped on sprang back up slowly.

Bryce found another cloth and started cleaning around the back of the caravan. Grit worked its way in under his nails, and wet spiderwebs wrapped around his fingers. He stopped and picked them off – they felt tough but they were so thin they were almost impossible to see. He could hear Kensa banging and muttering to herself.

'What offer was it?' he said.

'I've told her it's a waste of time.' Kensa started on the side window, thumping the cloth over the glass in wide arcs. Bits of dirt flew across onto Bryce's feet.

'You don't have to stay,' he said. 'You could do something else. Go.'

'What?'

'You could go.'

The banging stopped for a moment.

'Something would come up,' Bryce said. 'You could figure it out as you went.'

'Like you?' Kensa said. Her cloth thumped again at the window.

~

202

'Stop following me.' Kensa turned back and waved her arms at Bryce. She was wearing her rolled-up overalls, and there were scabs and freckles like paint spatters up her thin legs. 'Go home.'

Bryce slowed down but didn't stop. He kicked at the dusty path. 'You're going too far,' he said.

Kensa crossed over to the cliffs and looked down. The sea was very dark and very grey. A mass of tangled wood and netting drifted past.

'You're going too far,' Bryce said again. 'We're not meant to.'

'We used to go down here all the time,' Kensa told him.

'No we didn't,' Bryce said. He realised too late that she meant her and Nate. She'd been circling their old routes for days now – skirting the fields, the path round the headland, the rocks below. She'd been staying out later and later, coming back just in time for dinner, with mud and bits of stone stuck to her hands. She would avoid their parents' questions, bend her head down to her plate and eat. She wouldn't look at Bryce.

Bryce stayed where he was. A seal dipped in the water and made a crying sound. It was hot and his T-shirt stuck to his skin. He waited until Kensa climbed back up. The next day she slipped out again before he was awake.

The spring wind blew in strange, sporadic gusts, like it was working itself up to something. The sky was leaden and low, but a shaft of sun broke through, sweeping across like a searchlight.

Bryce came out of the shower, an old towel wrapped around his waist, the smell of rusty pipes and chlorine in his wet hair. He'd managed to work the controls now so that the water came out mostly warm, apart from the last freezing jet at the end. He'd glanced in the mirror, realised his hair was long and tangled round his ears, his eyes bloodshot from lack of sleep. He needed to shave too – his cheeks and jaw were thick with dark bristles. He thought of himself aged nine; his arms were so thin he could reach behind the tumble dryer in the laundry block and find any dropped money.

He was just in the doorway when the woman from the bungalow came past. When she saw him she jumped, but she tried to hide it.

'Sorry,' he said. He kept hold of the towel. The wind went up there like a bastard.

'I wasn't expecting … I was looking for Kensa. Is she back yet?'

'Back?'

'Last night. I saw the torch. She's usually back by now.'

Bryce turned and looked at the caravan. The curtains were still shut.

'It's just something I need to ask her, about the house.' The woman was looking everywhere except at him. She studied a crack in the wall, the way a dandelion was bursting out of it. 'Tell her she doesn't have to come in, it's just those boxes she left in the loft – old clothes and household things, some of your stuff, I think – she said she'd clear them but she hasn't yet and I sort of need the space.' One of her hands was resting on her stomach, which curved out under her jumper. He hadn't noticed it before.

He shut the shower-block door. 'I'll tell her,' he said. He crossed the field. He'd thought Kensa was still asleep. Her curtains were across, her door was shut, how was he meant to know she wasn't in there? What did the woman say? She's usually back by now. He didn't know anything.

He was almost at his tent when Kensa came up from the path. She looked tired. Her boots were wet and she was carrying the torch.

Bryce unzipped his door but stayed where he was. 'Been out?' he said.

'I couldn't sleep.' She crouched down and started to tighten one of his ropes.

'Where'd you go?' he asked.

She pushed a peg further into the ground with her boot. 'This thing looks like it's going to blow away any second.' She worked her boot so the peg was right in. 'I could see it bending as I came up.'

'Where'd you go?' Bryce said.

Kensa went back round the tent, checking each peg, each rope. 'You have to be careful pitching here,' she said. 'Because of the rocks. The pegs don't catch. You think the tent's secure but in a gale it'll just skid right across the field.' She banged at another peg with her heel until it disappeared into the ground.

Bryce nodded. When she was crouched down like that, he could see how sloped her shoulders were – it looked as if she was hunching against cold weather. The hoops of her earrings clinked softly against each other.

'You must have gone pretty far,' he said.

'I guess.'

'Out past the fields?'

'I guess.'

'Is that burnt-out barn still there?'

'What barn?'

'Further out that way, past the fields.'

'I don't know.'

'You would have seen it, if you went that way,' Bryce said. An ant started to crawl up his leg and he leaned down and brushed it off. 'We used to go there. The roof was collapsing. It would make these cracking noises, where the wood was about to give in.'

'I don't remember.'

'It was over that way.'

Kensa frowned. She pulled the canvas so that it was taut over the frame. 'Are you sure?'

'What do you mean am I sure?' Bryce said. There was a dull ache behind his eyes. He needed coffee, or a drink, maybe both. 'We used to go there.' As soon as he said it, he remembered the barn was somewhere else; by the road near the first place he'd lived when he moved away. He'd climbed onto the roof one night and felt the soft wood almost give way under him.

'Maybe,' Kensa said. 'I think I remember. Out past the fields?'

Bryce nodded. 'Yeah,' he said. 'Over there.'

Kensa finished with his tent and Bryce went inside to get dressed. He lay on his sleeping bag and put his head on the rolled-up jumper he was using as a pillow. The tent was so thin he could almost see through it. He took everything out of his bag and looked over it: jeans, socks, spare shirts, a phone with no battery, no signal. His wallet. A receipt for petrol. He put it all back carefully.

~

Bryce's bedroom door opened and a crack of light from the hallway grew and spread over the floor, and across his bed. There were footsteps, the stifled sound of breathing, and then Kensa was standing over him.

'I know where he went,' she said.

Bryce opened one eye. His clock read midnight. It was dark and quiet. He closed his eye and tried to tell Kensa to go away, but his mouth wouldn't work properly. He pulled the covers over his head.

'Come on,' Kensa whispered. She opened Bryce's wardrobe, pulled out some clothes for him and threw them onto the bed.

'Whatnma?' Bryce said.

'We have to go.'

Bryce sat up and rubbed over his eyes. His chin dropped onto his chest and he tried to lift it back up, but couldn't do it.

'I don't know why I didn't think of this before,' Kensa was saying. 'He kept talking about going down there. He wanted to go right to the back; he thought there might be bats, or maybe those glow-worms he'd read about. He couldn't find them anywhere else and he really wanted to see them. All he wanted to do was see them.'

Bryce watched as she moved around the room, pushing at her fringe and adjusting the batteries in the torch.

'Where?' he said. 'Where did he talk about?'

'The sea caves. I already said that. We have to go there now.'

'We're not allowed.' The caves were meant to be huge and pitch-black – you could walk in deeper and deeper and never come out. No one knew how far they stretched back.

'We have to go,' Kensa said.

Bryce sat back on the bed and folded his arms. 'You told me to go home.'

'When?'

'You told me to go home.' He lay back down and rolled himself in the duvet, leaving just enough of a gap so he could see what Kensa was doing.

She came over to the bed and stood right in front of him. She pressed again at the batteries in the torch and the light came on, the beam tilting upwards into her chin, making her eyes look huge and roving. 'You have to come,' she said.

Bryce didn't move. The duvet muffled his voice. 'Why?'

Kensa moved over to the window and looked out. 'Because.'

Bryce rolled himself tighter into the covers.

'I need you to come,' she said. 'OK?' She wouldn't turn around.

Bryce got up and put on his shoes.

Kensa opened the window and started climbing out. She balanced her feet on the windowsill then jumped over the spiky bushes in the flower bed.

Bryce followed behind. 'He took his sleeping bag though,' he whispered. 'And his mat. Why would he have taken those down there?' He tried to jump from the window, but slipped, and grabbed at the bottom of the palm tree, scratching his hands on the gristly bark.

'Ssshh,' Kensa said. She turned the torch off and threaded her way through the campsite. It was full and they had to go between tents and ropes, past the sounds of people sleeping and awnings lifting in the wind. There were hushed, gurgling snores, as if a plug was loose in a bath. A little kid called something out in his sleep. A dog barked and they froze, waiting for someone to come out and see them, but no one came. They kept going. Once they were past the tents and into the first field, Kensa turned the torch back on.

There was a thin moon and the clouds crowded around it like moths. The barley bent in the wind. They walked in silence, Kensa first, Bryce behind, his legs heavy, his mouth dry, trying to stop himself turning back with every step.

They crossed the edge of the field, then climbed the gate. Something rustled on the ground, then darted away. Kensa turned round to look at Bryce. The buckles on her sandals rattled softly and the moon striped her face with silver. She looked different somehow, like his sister but also not like his sister at all. As they carried on along the path he reached out to touch her, to check, but just as he was about to do it, his hand fell away.

The path turned stony and started to drop down towards the sea. The gritty dust scraped with each step, waves cracked against the rocks like beaten rugs, and there was something else as well – a strange, low noise, that Bryce had never noticed before – a sort of deep booming that echoed through the cliff and up into his feet. He stumbled on the stony path, righted himself, then stumbled again.

'Kensa?' he said.

'We're almost there.'

'What's that noise?'

'What?'

'That.'

'It's the caves,' Kensa said.

The sound got louder until it was all Bryce could hear. It beat in his ears like a sail. He skidded and stones rolled; he couldn't find anywhere stable to put his feet so he stopped and stood very still. He couldn't see Kensa. He couldn't move forward. It was so dark. He couldn't tell where the path was any more, where anything was.

'Kensa?' he whispered.

There was no answer.

The sea was booming in the caves, knocking against the walls. It sounded like his heart against his chest. It was dangerous to go in; it was too dark, the tide was too high. Water might be pushing in through the tunnels. He turned and looked back. There were a few tiny glints of light from the campsite. He took another step forward, then turned again. There was a scrabbling noise from the path below and the torch's beam swept up across the rocks.

'Wait for me,' Bryce called. 'Wait there. I'm coming down, OK?' He waited until he was sure Kensa had stopped, then he turned and ran back to the campsite to get their parents.

~

The storm came in suddenly. Bryce had just slipped into an uneasy sleep – dreaming of stones rolling, the moon, Kensa's muffled cry of surprise, her eyes narrowing, her face turning away. He woke with the side of his tent pushing against his mouth, water sluicing down his legs, the tent poles bowing like they were about to snap.

He sat up, got dressed, then tried to unzip his tent to go out, but the force of the wind and the rain drove him back in. He lay back down, felt the storm wrenching at the tent, trying to drag it across the grass. The poles strained. There was a tightness in the air, and then the lightning started, fast and bright, scattering across the sky like gunshots. The thunder came straight after, pealing like huge bells, and below it all was the relentless booming of the caves – he could almost feel them reverberating up the earth and into his back, the sea pummelling at the stone, hurling itself around the hollow tunnels, right under the campsite, under his tent, under everything.

He didn't know how long the storm lasted. Gradually the wind eased, gradually the rain thinned to mizzle. Everything in the tent was drenched: his sleeping bag, his wallet, his clothes. He unzipped the door and went out. It was just getting light.

The grass was flattened. There were leaves and twigs everywhere, bits of wood, a rusty hinge that had been bowled down from the gate. His tent hadn't moved – the ropes were still tight, the pegs still deep in the ground – but the main pole had snapped and one of the walls had ripped, making the sides crumple inwards like old fruit. There was a fine layer of sand along the roof.

He looked over at the caravan. The curtains were shut, the door was open and swinging in the wind. Bryce looked at his tent, his stuff, his car. Maybe he should just go. Maybe it would be easier if he just went.

He packed his sodden bag, walked to the car, and put it in the boot. He opened the door and sat in the driver's seat. He didn't turn on the engine. He sat for a long time. Then he got out and started walking.

He took the path down to the caves. Halfway there he looked down and saw Kensa. She was sitting on the rocks at the side of the path, staring at the sea. The tide was out. The water was creased and battered after the storm, brown with churned sand and teeming with choppy waves. The path was wet, the stones stained with rain. They rolled under his feet as he made his way down.

'Did you hear them?' Kensa said. 'They were so loud.'

'What are they like inside?'

Kensa zipped her coat tighter and watched the waves. 'I don't know.'

Bryce looked down at the rocks and the beach. He thought of Kensa crossing the fields, going down to the rocks, standing outside the caves, but never going in. He thought of her on the path that night, in the dark, waiting for him.

'Come on,' he said.

He made his way down, slipping on grit, clutching at wet rocks, Kensa following behind until they were on the beach. The caves were in front of them – there was a deep gap in the cliff that widened out into the dark, the stone shattered and polished by the sea as it shouldered its way further in.

Bryce walked up the beach and stood at the caves' mouth. Tunnels arched ahead of him, echoing and gleaming like a cathedral.

Kensa stood next to him. She had one hand deep in her pocket, the other was clutching the torch. 'What if we ...' she said, but she didn't finish.

The longer Bryce stared into the cave, the darker it looked. He took a step forward, his boots rattling on stones and bits of slate. He took another step and the slate became smooth, pale sand. He took a breath and walked in.

The air was cool and musty. After a moment, Kensa came in and turned on the torch, shining it on the dripping walls, which glistened black and red as if a flame had passed across them.

They walked forwards slowly. The walls dripped, the waves broke on the rocks very far away. Something moved above them, then a bat dropped down, circled the tunnel, and flew back up into the dark. Kensa moved ahead. Bryce picked his way through carefully, thinking of Nate's small torch, the way he used to keep it on all night, the worn straps on his rucksack, the look he had that Bryce now recognised, of someone who'd got used to moving on and not looking back.

The caves went deeper and the silence seemed to grow and thicken. There was no way of knowing which direction he was going – he just kept going, following the caves as they dipped and turned, breathing in the thin air. Sometimes the tunnels narrowed, sometimes they opened out like rooms. After a while he realised he couldn't hear Kensa any more. He couldn't see the torch. He stopped. There was no sound, no movement.

He waited in the tunnel. He didn't know how many turns he'd taken, how far or how deep he'd gone. He reached out and touched the wall, tried not to think of the miles of cliff all around him, the sea slowly making its way back in.

He held onto the cold stone. He called out. He waited. A stone clattered down and landed by his boot. Another bat dropped and circled. Then, finally, he heard footsteps in the distance. He let go of the wall and made his way towards the sound, stretching out his hands. He called again. His heart was pounding like the tide against the caves; the skin on his palms was damp and tingling. He half-expected to hear Kensa counting slowly down to zero. Any minute now she would stretch out her hands and find him.

Kensa called out, telling him to wait, to stay where he was, she'd be there in a minute, but he kept going. They could hear each other's footsteps, their breathing, they were getting closer, it was so dark, there were so many twists and bends, but any moment now they would find each other, any moment now they would know exactly where they were.

By-the-Wind Sailors

Marine organisms with an internal float and sail. The sail is either angled to the right or to the left. The sailor has no control over where it is blown by the wind – if the wind changes direction, the sailor may get pushed inland and stranded.

At the end of winter they move to a caravan. The site is on a cliff and easterlies cut across like scythes. There is a reception and a laundry area and a row of slot machines. On Saturday nights the disco floods music over the sea. There is the sound of waves constantly, and gulls, and the two-a.m. couple who chase each other around the fields full of wrath, then make up again inside, shouting out their remorse, bottles and tins rattling against the window. Some mornings there is frost crackling the grass. Other mornings the sun lays out warmth in copper sheets. The thrift is just starting to bloom. The sand martins arrive back to nest in the crumbling cliffs.

The family are Ruby and Nathan Tulley and their daughter Lacey. Ruby is short and gaunt and never keeps still – she bites her lips, pulls out eyelashes, gnaws at the skin around her nails.

Her hair is dyed maroon but it has faded to dusty purple, like the colour of sloes before they are ripe. She met Nathan at a garage sale, both of them buying someone else's chipped plates and flat cushions. Nathan is a sleepy man, and so shy that he hides if he sees anyone he knows. His skin is dry and red but he doesn't like to use the cream that Ruby got for him – it stings – so every night he gently squeezes some into the sink and turns on the tap.

He fixes fences and gates and anything else that comes his way. Ruby can sew better than anyone and she takes in dresses and shirts and works on them on her second-hand Singer, a thistle-head of pins stored in the corner of her mouth. Lacey sits very still under chairs and tables, sticks her tongue between the gap in her teeth, and doesn't say much at all.

There are a hundred static caravans and it's not the busy season, but somehow they end up in one right on the edge of the site, a mile from the facilities and half-tilted into a sloppy furrow. The front window is cracked and the curtains and walls are adorned with mould and midges. All the shine has been scoured off the plyboard. But it's dry enough inside and there's a small, neat table with three wicker chairs, which turn out to be a lot more comfortable than they look. Ruby and Nathan sit on theirs, Lacey sits under hers. There is a pattern of white leaves and cigarette burns on the carpet.

There was a fire at the flat they'd been renting in town, so they only have a few singed bags with them. The whole building went up overnight and by morning was nothing more than crumpled bricks, plaster and melted plastic. The family can't remember how they got out. Sometimes they go back over it but none of them can remember anything about getting out. One moment there was the reek and pressure of smoke, and the next they were standing on the street watching reams of yellow tape twisting in the wind, and blue lights flashing. They didn't know where to go. Then Ruby remembered how she and Nathan had stayed in a caravan for a few months after they'd got married. It had been a good time. There was no heating, so they would do their laundry in the evenings and then sit with the warm bags on their laps, drinking beer by the mugful.

But in this caravan they never seem to get warm. Nathan can't shake off a rattling cough and tightness in his lungs. Ruby scrubs the mould off the curtains but it keeps creeping back. There is always a strange, smoky smell on their clothes that won't wash out. Lacey takes to lying flat underneath the loose carpet. She's so small that Ruby sometimes stands on her by accident. Everything is broken and it's impossible to get hold of the site's owner, so Nathan fixes the beds and the overhead cupboards and Ruby prises out the black gunge between the tiles in the shower. Slowly, they find a routine. The chairs are the best thing in the whole place and they look forward to the end of the day when they can sit quietly in them. They lean back against the creaking wicker and close their eyes. I guess you can get used to anywhere, they say to each other. Nathan goes out early to the farm where he is repairing the fences. Ruby watches Lacey and mends the caravan's torn bedding and curtains. She's hoping that once they can get hold of the owner, he might give her the work of the whole site.

When the wind squalls, the caravan rocks from side to side. One godawful night it feels as if it's sliding down the field towards the sea. They run out into the dark and throw bricks in front of it. Nathan digs a deep trench and goes back to bed muddy. In the morning, there is no sign that the caravan has moved at all. Lacey strings a row of things she's found along the back window. There are bits of coal, wet feathers, and a clutch of plastic key rings, salt-scrubbed but still bright, covered in writing no one can read because it's in Mandarin.

In the middle of summer, more tourists come and the park is full. Nathan says that people look over at their caravan kind of funny but Ruby knows what Nathan is like. Really, he's glad that no one tries to speak to them. The hotplate is working better now, and the damp is drying out. In the mornings, the skylarks rise up into the air as if on ladders.

Then, one afternoon, they come back and find their door flung wide open. There's a man inside painting the walls. He has headphones on, and he whistles, glances round, then gets back to work. He paints straight over the mould and the midges, so that there are tiny bumps where they've been sealed in. It seems that their caravan is now needed as overflow for the holiday season, and they realise with a jolt that in the panic of finding somewhere to live they'd signed no contracts, been given no guarantees. Ruby goes to find the owner to demand an explanation but it's impossible to get hold of him.

They move to an annexe in town. It's almost the end of summer. The geese fly back from their breeding grounds inland. The annexe belongs to a man who is recently separated. At first his wife slept in the spare bedroom, then she lived in the annexe and then she moved out completely. She obviously wanted to do it in stages. When the family move in, the annexe is, as Ruby says, cold enough to freeze the balls off a swinging cat. Northerlies blow straight through the thin walls. There are still some of the wife's things lying around. Next to the bed, there's a shelf with her glasses on, a half-open book and a mug of freezing tea. Ruby tips the tea away, then puts everything in a bag and puts the bag under the bed. Under the bed there is a white shoe and a tightly rolled-up newspaper. Nathan finds her toothbrush by the sink. Lacey puts on a pair of silver clip-on earrings.

It's not a bad place: the window looks out over a chestnut tree and they find a brittle pack of cards in a drawer and teach Lacey to play blackjack and shithead. But sometimes the husband wanders in without knocking and paces through the small rooms. Or he sits on the sofa for a long time, doing nothing but staring at the wall. The family stay very quiet and retreat into the kitchen. Then only Nathan's coughing seems to startle him into getting up and going away.

The bag under the bed fills up. They find her hairbrush under the sofa, a T-shirt folded against the back of a drawer. The bathroom smells of her spicy perfume. Ruby finds Lacey under the bed, looking through the wife's book and frowning. The husband starts coming in more and more but now he is busy doing things: he paints the walls and does something to stop the damp coming through. The house smells of paint and clean carpets. They don't like it; they don't like the smell of the paint or the way he whistles as he's working. Why didn't he do all this last autumn, when they first moved in? They watch and wait. One day draught-proofing appears round the windows; another day there's a picture hanging above the sofa. Ruby shakes her head and bites at the skin around her nails. The picture is too much. They are already half-packed when the wife comes in, laden with bags. The husband is right behind her. The wife puts down her suitcase and looks around the room. It was never going to be for ever, she says.

The next place is a cabin at the bottom of an overrun garden. Bindweed chokes the windows. There are spiderwebs over the door. Every morning a gull taps rhythmically on the glass with its beak. It wants the flash of silver on the sink's plug, but can never seem to get any closer. The cabin was built for children who now prefer to spend their time drinking White Lightning in pool clubs and sand dunes. It's almost as big as the annexe, but the beds are narrow built-in bunks – something they didn't notice at first and now it's too late. At night, Ruby leans down from her bunk and watches Nathan and Lacey sleeping. Sometimes she reaches down and touches them gently on their shoulders.

There are dark shapes on the walls where pictures used to be stuck – shapes of birds and rainbows imprinted on the fading wood. There is a crap dolphin that looks more like a canoe. On good days, the cabin is warm and there is the sweet tang of pine trees. On bad days, the pine trees block out the sun, the windows steam up and drip onto the bunks, the tiny fridge shudders and stops, and there is the uneasy sound of gunshots from nearby fields. There are more bad days than good ones.

What follows is a dire stint in a shoddily divided house, crammed in with two families who seem to thrive on cacophony: yowling dogs, labyrinthine disputes, endless music broadcast from phones and laptops. The house has been split into three but to get to their rooms upstairs they have to go along the hallway of the downstairs flat, and across the kitchen of the middle one. The dogs go off whenever they open the kitchen door, and there are often parties that are so sudden and surging that it's impossible for Ruby and Nathan to get through them. Once they are trapped in the hall for two hours, until Ruby works out a way of getting in via a half-open upstairs window. Lacey stops going to bed, and instead lies on the floor, watching the parties through a crack in the boards. It's a dismal few months, and they feel more embroiled in the lives of the two families than they do in their own; but they've learned the words to all the songs by Elvis; how to calm an agitated greyhound; how to pass through rooms and doorways without being noticed at all.

They spend a few weeks in an empty bed and breakfast, with a landlady who cannot sleep and who soothes herself by walking up and down the stairs, her knees clicking like dice. Then another week in a dilapidated roadside hotel; another in a dim room above a pub, with a strange oil painting of a stag on the wall, which vibrates to the jukebox and the mirth and the brawls.

Living out of bags that must be packed and unpacked constantly is, they soon realise, a complete bastard, so they decide to go back to the caravan. The one they stayed in before

221

is available again; for some reason no one else wants it. The geese move back inland for the summer. Inside, the paint is still almost fresh. The crack in the front window has been fixed. A single hotplate that is theirs and theirs alone is a sudden luxury, a miracle even. It's warm – the wind has shifted and is coming from the south. Lacey sits outside and plays solitaire with the cards she took from the annexe. Ruby sticks up adverts for her sewing. Work has been slow for her recently but Nathan is always busy – he goes out early in the mornings and works his way back and forth along the fences on the outer farms. There is always broken fencing. At night his cough is no louder than the breeze that pushes in around the door.

Then winter comes. At first they think they'll be able to manage. They get hold of an extra duvet and some thick material to line the curtains. In the evenings, they warm their hands over the hotplate. I guess you can get used to anything, they say to each other. But it's a ruthless winter. The windows freeze on the inside. The three of them huddle in one bed. Lacey keeps waking up and saying she can hear a gull tapping on the window. Nathan's cough gets worse. When Ruby finds mould growing on Lacey's jumper there's nothing left to do but pack up their bags.

It's not that hard to find a new place. Ruby has heard about a village just outside town, where the houses are full all summer, then empty all winter. Some of the houses are advertised as winter lets. The family move into a small cottage in a row of other small cottages. It's the kind of place they used to talk about living in one day. The doors are painted green and there's wisteria or clematis or whatever the hell it is growing all over them. The village is very quiet apart from the thrum of the sea in the distance. There's no sound from either of the houses next door: no footsteps on the stairs, no doors opening and closing. The curtains stay half-drawn. At night there are two lights from windows in the distance. Empty dustbins clatter in the wind.

For some reason they can't settle. A gate scrapes and Nathan goes out and fixes it. Now it's really quiet. Lacey wakes up in the night and thinks she's in the caravan. She goes into the hall and pees on the doormat. The fridge hums softly. The furniture and plates and curtains are almost too nice to touch and the family try not to touch them too much. They use the same three plates over and over. When Lacey breaks hers, Ruby shouts: shitting hell, Lacey, those are good plates. She tries to stick it together but it doesn't stick. Lacey goes and sits under the table and Nathan sits with her.

One evening, the house alarm goes off when Nathan comes in from work. They try to stop it but the electrics are complicated. After twenty minutes it turns off, but for a long time afterwards Ruby and Nathan pace and look out of the windows. It happens again the next night, and the next. They sit in the kitchen with their hands over their ears as the alarm blares over the village.

After six weeks there's a message on the answerphone. A woman's voice bellows a greeting to the house's owners: she's glad that they've finally decided to come down for Christmas, they should let her know as soon as they arrive so that she can drop round and see them. Should she bring trifle or mousse? The red light on the phone blinks. Nathan plays the message again. He doesn't like mousse or trifle. It's the first they've heard of the owners coming down. There were no timeframes when they moved in, but surely winter lasts until at least February. Ruby curses the owners in long and complicated ways. Nathan says that maybe they'll have to stay in a bed and breakfast and then come back once the house is empty again. But all the bed and breakfasts are booked and double the price around this time of year. They don't have to rush – they've got over four weeks to work something out, but they want to go as quickly as possible; they don't want to leave it so late that they have to witness the owner's arrival, the awkward crossover in the doorway.

They pack up. They can't remember why they used to imagine living in such a place; they can't connect that old dream with themselves at all. The alarm wails out one more time as they go. Lacey sticks a finger up at it and doesn't get told off.

Nathan has found a place they can stay. A shop in town has a flat above it that's available. The shop sells CDs and records and rents out films. Ruby and Nathan used to go there a lot. They've lived above shops before and had a good time. In the day there is bustle but at night it's mostly quiet. Shops are always heated and the heat rises into the flats. There is one bedroom and the sofa in the living room folds out for Lacey. It's snug and grungy, with the smell of old cigarettes and cooking – just what they like. There's no worrying about expensive plates here. There are always footsteps and voices and cars, and bright lights along the road at night. The roof is porous and lets in westerlies, dandelion seeds, hibernating butterflies, the sound of the Friday-night drunks calling up the street like mournful geese.

But the shop gets steadily quieter. A few months pass, and then a year. One afternoon Ruby notices a sign outside that says 'Clearance Sale'. No one has mentioned anything to them. Apparently people aren't renting out films from shops any more. Ruby and Nathan can't help remembering all the times they used to go in and pick out a film, then post it back through the door on Sunday mornings. They don't understand why people would rather click a button and stay indoors. Sometimes it seems like the world is moving on without them. The stock in the shop empties and a 'For Sale' sign goes up. They spend a sad hour packing their bags. They fold the bed up into the sofa. Lacey rips a corner of wallpaper, writes something behind it and sticks it back down with spit.

There is nowhere else to go except back to the winter-let cottage. They unpack their bags. The snowglobe and the ornament of a shepherdess they had in the old flat don't look right here and end up banished to the back of a cupboard. The owners have left a half-eaten box of chocolates from their last Christmas visit and Ruby tries one. It's strawberry and stale. The gate Nathan fixed before seems to have bust again, and creaks quietly in the wind.

One night Lacey comes into their room and says she can smell fire. Nathan and Ruby rush downstairs and there's a smouldering ember from the stove on the carpet. They stamp it out for a long time, then stay up until morning, clutching each other's hands, watching the carpet for smoke. The ember has burned a black mark right through to the floorboards.

Winter ends and they wait for word from the landlords. But no word comes. Spring turns into summer and then winter again. Ruby spends an afternoon ringing up to find their post – they are due final bills from old rentals, bank statements and God knows what else. Automated messages tell her the same thing each time: her details can't be located and will need to be found and looked into. The messages always promise that someone will get back to her. They start receiving supermarket offer sheets almost every day, addressed to old tenants and old owners of the house. Lacey draws circles around all the things she wants: half-price lemonade, bin liners, pasta shaped into thin, contorted faces.

They stop thinking of moving. Nathan puts up a shelf in the bathroom. Ruby paints one wall of the kitchen blue. Lacey lines up snail shells along her bedroom window. At night there are no other lights, and it's the calling of owls, not beer lorries or people or discos, that makes its way through the windows. The gate scrapes in the wind. They sleep lighter and wake much earlier than usual. The days become much longer. One night they see a meteor shower that rends the sky with silver. I guess you can get used to anywhere, they say to each other. After all, it's the most beautiful place they have ever lived – surely it's ridiculous to feel unsure about it, to miss the thump of music on Saturday nights, the smell of old cigarettes, the strange darkness of pine trees.

Overnight, the cottage sells. There hasn't even been a 'For Sale' sign outside but Nathan says he supposes it was all done over the internet. They've never got round to owning a computer or an expensive phone. Sometimes it seems like the world is moving on without them. Estate agents and surveyors prowl around. Nathan takes down the shelf and they paint over the blue wall in the kitchen. The wooden counters and draining board are bleached with watermarks and they spend a terrified few hours trying to scrub them off. What kind of sadist has a draining board you can't get wet? Ruby says. She had learned to love that stupid wood. They rub a damp teabag along it to stain the watermarks brown and make them blend back in. It seems to work. Slowly and systematically they erase themselves from the house. Nathan unpins Lacey's drawings and fills in the holes. Ruby patches up the burn mark in the carpet and does it so well that it looks as if they have never been there at all.

They move back to the caravan. It's the end of winter. They miss stairs and, for a while, a single hotplate does not seem like enough. The wicker chairs are as comfortable as ever. Nathan adjusts the table so they can all fit round it and play with the deck of cards. They are teaching Lacey whist, and arseholes and presidents. The wind cuts across the cliff like a scythe. Some days it brings with it the coconut smell of the gorse. Some days it rocks the caravan like a bloody cradle. They put bricks either side to balance it out. Really, you can get used to anywhere, they say to each other.

Nathan goes out and mends the fences on a farm he worked on only a year before. It seems that fence posts nowadays are rotting out sooner and sooner. Ruby mends the frayed seats in the caravan and hums a song by Elvis. Lacey digs out the chunk of coal she buried three summers ago. It's just the same as she left it: glossy and heavy and exactly the same size as her palm.

The mildew on the caravan is creeping back, and the corner of the window has a hairline crack that looks to be spreading. The two-a.m. couple fight and make up again. The thrift is just beginning to bloom. The sand martins come back to nest in the crumbling cliffs.

Acknowledgements

THANK YOU TO MY agent Elizabeth Sheinkman and my editor Helen Garnons-Williams for their encouragement, advice and enthusiasm. Thank you to everyone at 4th Estate. Thank you to the Roger and Laura Farnworth Residency at Warleggan, which gave me two weeks to write in such peaceful and beautiful surroundings. Thank you to Jos Smith and Anneliese Mackintosh for their help and advice. Thank you to Mum. Thank you to Ben, as always, for everything.

Grateful acknowledgement is also due to Arts Council England, who supported this book with a writer's grant.